ELENA UNBOUND

OTHER WORLD SERIES BOOK SEVEN

RAMONA GRAY

EK PUBLISHING INC.

ELENA UNBOUND

OTHER WORLD SERIES BOOK SEVEN

Men rule.

Women eagerly submit… except Elena. She refuses to wear a man's collar and doesn't sleep around. Until a scarred stranger with a dangerous past rescues her.

Will one torrid night together be enough? Falling for a man of his station is a risk, and Traven's attention span for women who share his bed is fleeting.

Only she may have more to fear than a broken heart.

A traitor hides among them, and as Elena and Traven grow closer, the real threat lurks around every dark corner. Loyalties are tested. Truth is elusive.

Can the betrayer be found, or will true love be their death?

Note: This is Book Seven in the Other World Series. It is a stand-alone book in the series, and you DO NOT have to read Books One to Six before reading this one.

CHAPTER 1

The freezing rain lashed down, the rising wind made short work of the last of the dead leaves still clinging to their branches. As the wind became a howling, spinning, whirling rush of cold air, the smaller trees bent and snapped like twigs.

The darkness that blanketed the land ebbed away. Not from the rising of the sun, but from the small orb of light that hovered just above the forest floor. It grew larger, as electricity crackled, and a low hum broke the silence.

Thunder boomed across the night sky and a jagged flash of lightning struck the earth only inches from the orb. It grew larger and larger still, the light pulsating until it flashed so brightly, the forest was lit up for miles for the brief seven seconds it took for the orb to spit out the man.

He landed with a hard thud on the ground, a grunt of pain escaping his lips when he landed on his elbow. As the wind died down and the hard chips of rain slowed, the man sat up, rubbing his bruised elbow and squinting into the darkness.

"What the fuck?"

Okay, so this was bad. Not like, got a flat tire on the freeway, bad. More like, about to die in the middle of some weird ass forest, bad.

John leaned against a pine tree, staring thoughtfully at a large, moss-covered rock just to his left. The pit of worry in his stomach swelled, he was almost certain he'd already seen that rock.

"Fuck," he muttered. "I'm going in goddamn circles."

He shoved his hands into the pocket of his jeans and yanked out his cell phone. It was dead. Had been ever since he'd been sucked in by that weird ball of light in the parking lot of his office building.

It wasn't dead before that. In fact, it was fully charged. He'd just used it to text Sasha about a booty call hookup. She'd been more than willing to have him stop by, despite the lateness of the hour.

He'd finished up the last of his paperwork, shoved his laptop into his desk and headed out. He'd been the last to leave the office, something that wasn't an unusual occurrence. Although, this time, not even the cleaning people were in the building. They'd finished up two hours before that.

The storm had grown steadily worse while he worked, and he'd stood under the awning for a bit, trying to wait out the rain. When it became obvious that it wasn't going to stop, he'd decided to make a run for it to his car. Afterall, Sasha was waiting, and she had promised him she'd be wearing that red little number that always made his dick hard.

He hadn't noticed the light at first, too consumed by the rain that pelted him and the rising wind that almost knocked him off his feet. When he'd finally noticed the circle of light, it was already twice the size of him. He'd been sucked into the weird, glowing orb like a dust bunny into a vacuum and then spit out in an honest-to-god forest.

He glanced around, peering up at the cold sunlight that was filtering through the trees. Unlike sunny California, this place was goddamn cold. So cold he could see his breath. Even if the weather wasn't freezing, he would have known he wasn't in California.

Call it intuition, or maybe just an innate sense of direction, but he definitely wasn't in his home state. Hell, he was pretty certain he wasn't even in America anymore.

"Siberia," he said. "Maybe I'm in Siberia."

Are you fucking crazy, John? So, you really think some flash of light just sucked you across the world?

You got any better ideas?

His inner voice did not, in fact, have any better ideas – at least its silence indicated it didn't - and he rubbed his bruised elbow absently as he studied the trees.

First things first – he had to get out of the fucking forest and find some civilization. He'd already spent one miserable night out here, huddling under some bushes like a frightened mouse until the sun had finally risen.

He was cold, he was hungry, and he was dehydrated. If he didn't find people soon…

He pushed that thought out of his head and pressed the power button on his cell phone. Nothing happened and he resisted the urge to just chuck it into the bushes. Maybe the flash of light had drained its battery and he just needed a damn charger for it.

He shoved it into his pocket and stood straight, grabbing onto the tree when he felt a little woozy. Okay, he could do this. He needed to find some higher ground, so that he could see what direction to walk before –

The woman's scream sent his blood whooshing through

3

his ears. He froze solid, his hand gripping the bark of the tree, his pulse pounding. The scream sounded like it came from his left and he pushed away from the tree and jogged in that direction.

Her second scream was louder, angrier. He could hear the low grunts of men and he jogged faster. He could see flashes of colour amongst the trees ahead and he broke into a run when he saw the man slap the woman across the face.

She fell to the ground and the man made a grunt of satisfaction. A second man was standing nearby, watching with a smug sort of amusement.

"Are you going to just stand there or help me?" The first man said as the woman jumped back to her feet.

The second gave him a sneering grin. "You cannot handle a woman, can you?"

"Hey, asshole!" John stopped behind the first man. "Get the fuck away from her, dickhead. She doesn't want -"

A sharp pain pierced his back and he suddenly felt like he was standing in a very warm puddle. He looked down, staring in disbelief at the rain of blood pattering out of his abdomen and the sharp tip of the sword sticking out just above his navel. The man behind him made a low grunt and shoved the sword in further, his hot breath washing over John's neck.

"Mind your business, stranger," the man said.

"H-help me," John whispered.

He stared at the woman. Her pale face was washed in horror and she gave him a helpless look as the man behind him yanked the sword out from his back.

His legs suddenly too weak to support him, John fell to his knees, his hands pressing against his stomach in an attempt to stop the blood that was pouring out from him.

"Help me," he whispered again. "A doctor, I need a…"

Darkness was edging his vision and as it overtook him

completely, the last thing he saw was the woman's horrified face.

THE SCREAMS THAT ECHOED THROUGH THE FOREST MADE Traven's horse snort nervously and the hair on the back of his neck stand up. The screams were full of rage and fear and he automatically rode toward them. He'd been travelling for many days and he was weary and ready to be in a bed again, but he couldn't ignore her screams.

As he grew closer, the woman screamed for a third time and there were louder grunts and growls of men. He dismounted, tied his horse to a tree and crept closer on foot. He peered around a large oak tree, and anger swept through him.

Two men with stained and ripped clothing were pinning a woman to the ground. She was thrashing and kicking furiously at them. Like most of the women from this area, she was tall with full breasts and wide hips. A small grin crossed his face when she suddenly bent her knees and kicked the man leaning over her, directly in the stomach.

Coughing and retching, he fell back as the man pinning her arms down roared with anger. The man she had kicked stood up and retched once more, spit flying from his mouth. With an angry snarl he fell on her, pulling at her heavy skirt.

She shrieked, the sound thin and birdlike in the cold air, and reared up, her back arching off the ground. He stepped out from behind the tree as the man on top of her balled his hand into a fist and punched her in the face. She slumped back against the ground, moaning dazedly and the two men grinned at each other.

"She's a feisty one."

"Aye. I love 'em that way too," the second man said. He reached for her full breasts. Before he could squeeze them, a sword appeared and tapped him lightly on his outstretched arm.

He looked up, his mouth dropping open to reveal black and rotting teeth. Before he could speak, Traven's fist smashed him directly in the mouth and he sagged to the ground, teeth and blood flying from his mouth.

The other man jumped to his feet, reaching for his own sword.

"I would advise against that." Traven held his sword loosely in one large fist.

The man hesitated and then grabbed at the handle of his sword. He gave a small gasp of surprise, looking down to see Traven's sword buried deeply in his belly.

"What?" he whispered.

Traven yanked the sword out and watched disinterestedly as the smaller man fell to the ground, blood pouring from his stomach. The stranger died quietly, his mouth gaping like a fish.

He put his sword away and turned to the woman. She was still lying on the ground and moaning softly. He bent over her and she pushed weakly at him. "Do not touch…"

Her eyes rolled up in her head and her head sagged to the side as she passed out.

Traven kicked the unconscious man in the hip, and he moaned but didn't wake. There was a third man, dead as well, lying only a few feet away. Traven glanced briefly at the woman before stepping over the unconscious man and walking forward. He knelt next to the dead man, staring curiously at him.

"What manner of clothing is this?" He touched the heavy material of the man's pants. It was thick and a dark blue in colour and even if they weren't soaked in blood, Traven thought they looked heavy and cumbersome to wear. The dead man's shirt had no buttons in the front and his jacket…

Traven touched the material of the man's jacket before examining the strange metal tab with its strange metal teeth. He'd never seen anything like it before and he stared at the dead man for almost five minutes before standing.

He thought briefly of searching the man's pockets, then decided against it. What was the use? He was dead and could give him no information. The wind was growing colder, and if he lingered much longer, the woman would be frozen to the bone. He took one last glance at the man before returning to the woman.

He picked her up with a loud grunt, carried her through the trees to his horse and steadied her on it before swinging into the saddle behind her. He pulled a short piece of rope from a saddle bag and lashed her wrists to the saddle horn before pushing her back against his wide chest. Her head lolled on his shoulder until with a soft snort, her face fell into the curve of his thick neck. He dug his heels into the sides of his horse and continued on his way.

ELENA BURIED HER FACE AGAINST THE MAN'S WARM SKIN before pressing a soft kiss against it. Her cheek was hurting as was the back of her head and she frowned in thought. Why did it hurt? Had she fallen? She kissed his warm, hard flesh again, sighing happily when his arm slid around her waist and pulled her closer. God, she'd missed a man's touch. His hand was stroking her ribs just below her breasts and she arched her back encouragingly. How long had it been since she felt a man's hand cupping her breast? Too long.

A part of her knew this was a dream, knew that she was alone in her cold bed, but she suddenly desperately wanted it to be real. It felt real – the man's breath washing over her cheek and neck was bringing goosebumps to her skin and his hand was heavy and delightfully warm against her side. The swaying of the bed was a bit strange, but she ignored that part. She wanted to be touched, to be reminded that she was a woman with needs and desires that had been ignored for far too long.

"Please," she whispered before nipping at his neck.

The man inhaled sharply before squeezing her side. "Wake up, girl."

She frowned and shook her head before kissing his neck again.

"Girl, open your eyes."

His rough voice demanded obedience and she reluctantly dragged her eyelids up. She squinted at the light trickling through the trees before she straightened. She could see her breath and the breath of the horse that she was riding on.

Her eyes widened as she remembered where she was and what had happened. She'd been captured by the horrible men in the forest. Her hands were bound to the saddle horn and, panic rushing through her, she turned her head to bite the throat of her captor.

He was quick, she'd give him that. His hand wrapped in her hair and held tight, preventing her from sinking her teeth into his throat.

"Enough, little minx. While I enjoyed your sweet love bites, I do not believe that is your intention now, is it?"

She flushed bright red, her grey eyes darkening to slate as he tugged her head up so he could study her face. It wasn't one of the men who had captured her in the forest but that didn't mean she wasn't in trouble.

"Where are the other men?"

He shrugged. "One is dead, the other will live if he wakes before the animals of the forest dine on him."

She yanked at the rope that bound her wrists. His horse snorted and jigged to the left, and he put his heavily-muscled arm around her waist and pulled her back against him. "Be still, you are spooking my horse. Relax, you are safe now. I will not harm you."

She looked around and then tugged at her restraint again. "Why am I tied up?"

"I was worried you would think I was one of the men in the woods and struggle. I did not want you tumbling from the horse and breaking your neck."

"I am not going to struggle. You can untie me."

"Aye, I could."

He made no move to untie the rope and she sighed with frustration. "Please?"

"What is your name?"

"Elena."

"Why were you in the woods alone, Elena?"

"I was not alone. I was travelling with two companions. Those men attacked us and killed them." She cleared her throat. "I ran, but they caught me. They killed another, a stranger who appeared out of nowhere. He-he wore very odd clothing."

"Aye, I saw him." The man didn't seem to be that interested in the dead man's clothes. "These companions – were they your lovers?"

She twisted around to glare at him. "What? No, they were not my lovers."

"Then why were you with them?"

"We were travelling for supplies for my employer."

"Whose home do you belong to?"

"The lord Enderson's."

He tensed against her, and she glanced at him. "Do you know him?"

"Aye, in a manner of speaking." He shrugged his cloak from one arm. She stared at the armband that announced his allegiance to the lord Enderson. The blue and gold was a startling contrast against the drab brown of his shirt.

"You are one of his men. Are you returning from the war?"

"Aye."

"So, it is true, the war is over." She glanced at him again. "What of the lord Enderson? Does he still live?"

"Why do you ask that?"

"Because the rumour is that he died in the last days of the war. Did he?"

"No. He will be home shortly."

She mulled that over for a moment. "Lord Barten will be thrilled."

He frowned at the obvious sarcasm in her voice. "What do you mean by that, girl?"

"Nothing." She stared up at him again. He was one of the largest men she'd ever seen, which was saying a lot considering how big the men were in this area. His face was nearly hidden behind a long, bushy beard and his hair was past his shoulders. It was wild and thick, the sides held back with a small piece of leather, and she could see small bits of leaves stuck in it.

She could barely see his mouth beneath the overgrown beard, but she had no problem seeing the scar that started at his hairline and coursed down his face, disappearing beneath the thick coating of hair that covered his jaw. It had just missed his left eye and she flushed a little when she realized he was staring at her mouth, his light green eyes darkening with an emotion she easily recognized.

Quickly, she turned around, her heart beating frantically in her chest, as he bent his head into her throat and inhaled deeply.

"You smell good, girl." His voice had deepened into a thick purr. Whether it was his voice or the way his hard hand was rubbing her belly slowly and gently, an ache, one that she had thought was gone forever, started up in her lower belly.

"Thank you, my lord." She cleared her throat nervously. "Would you please untie me now?"

"It has been a long time since I have been this close to a woman." He placed a gentle kiss on her throat.

She shivered, ignoring the surprising pleasure she felt at the touch of his mouth against her skin, "Do you always grope women you have just met, my lord?"

"Not always."

She bit back the laughter at his reply. She was shocked by her sudden need for the man who had saved her life. Was it because she had come so close to being raped and murdered by the men in the woods? Was her relief at being unharmed, thanks to the man behind her, bringing out her need? Or simply the fact that she'd been alone for so long? She had no idea, but it would not do to give him even a hint that she was finding his touch pleasing.

He slid his hand up her ribcage and very carefully cupped her breast with one large hand, rubbing his thumb over the nipple.

"You should stop, my lord. You saw what happened to the last men who touched me by force." She hated how breathless and needy she sounded. She didn't want to be attracted to him.

He grunted. "Aye, I did. You are lucky I showed up when I did."

"I would have been fine." She blushed a little at her obvious and foolish lie.

He laughed, a rich, warm sound that made her entire body tingle. "Aye, perhaps. You did seem rather adept at kicking."

"Although," he said as her traitorous nipple hardened under his touch, "it does not feel like I will need to use force."

He kissed her neck again before kissing his way to her ear and sucking lightly on her earlobe. His beard tickled and a little moan escaped her mouth.

When he pulled on the string that laced her shirt closed, she told herself to object, to demand he not touch her. Instead, she arched her back invitingly as he unlaced it and pulled her shirt open, exposing her bare breasts to both his gaze and the cool air. He inhaled sharply at the sight of her large firm breasts. Her pink nipples hardened in the cold as he put his heavy thighs over hers, pinning her legs down against the sides of his horse.

His horse snorted and sidestepped a bit and he patted it on the side of its large neck. It calmed and continued to pick its way through the trees as he cupped her left breast. He kneaded it gently before pulling on her nipple, smiling with satisfaction at her soft moan.

He switched to the right breast, cupping and rubbing and lightly pinching her nipple until her back was arching. She turned her face toward him, pressing her lips against his. He immediately angled his mouth over hers and kissed her hard. She opened her mouth wide so that he could explore it with his tongue. He flicked his tongue against hers and when she timidly slipped her tongue into his mouth, he sucked hard on it, making her moan.

He dropped the reins and used both hands to cup her breasts. He squeezed and rubbed them, pulling with rough fingers on both her nipples, and rubbing his crotch against her ass as she sighed and moaned. He licked her neck before sucking hard on it. He made a soft noise of satisfaction deep in his throat.

"You seem to be enjoying my touch, sweet Elena," he murmured into her ear.

The sound of his deep voice broke the haze of desire that had enveloped her, and she squirmed against him, blushing furiously. What was she doing? She didn't even know his name.

Humiliated by her reaction to the stranger and her inability to resist his touch, she lied to him. "My lord, I belong to another. If he finds out that you -"

"Where is your collar?"

"I do not wear a collar. My – my man is secure enough that he does not require me to wear one."

He laughed. "No man lets his woman go without a collar. If she shares his bed, she wears the collar that tells other men she belongs to him."

"He does not believe in such barbaric practices. He understands that women are not property to be -"

She gasped when he slipped his hand under the waistband of her skirt and cupped her pussy. He gave a grunt of surprise at the feel of the soft hair between her legs.

"Why do you have hair here?" He asked, his fingers stroking the soft curls.

"Because I am a woman and not a little girl," she snapped. She tried to move her legs out from under his, but it was impossible. He used his legs to push her legs back, spreading them further apart and giving him better access to her warmth.

He rubbed a bit of her hair between his fingers, "Why do you not do what the other women do and remove it?" He asked.

"Why should I? Because you would prefer it? It is my body and I refuse to remove all the hair just to please a man."

TRAVEN GRINNED TO HIMSELF. ELENA HAD SPIRIT AND HE loved how she reacted to his touch. He stroked the hair that covered her pussy again. After years of being with women who were shaved, or plucked, or waxed completely bare, the feel of her soft curls was an exciting change. His cock was so hard it was nearly painful, and he pressed it against her ass again. Her ass pressed back against him before she made a soft huff and glared at him.

He pressed a kiss against the tip of her nose as he looked around. It was growing darker and he would have to find shelter for them soon. He was close enough to home to recognize the area and he frowned briefly, trying to remember the layout of the land. If he was correct, there were a series of small caves not far from here. One of them would provide enough shelter for the evening.

He was still cupping her warm core, his fingers gently stroking the curls as she trembled against him. He hesitated and then made a sudden decision. If he gave her pleasure now, made her come, she would be more open to the idea of letting him fuck her later. He was going to fuck her tonight, he knew that as well as he knew his own name, but he wanted her warm and willing. Showing her how easily he could make her come would be the fastest way to make that happen.

He slid his index finger between her pussy lips and found her clit. He rubbed it with firm pressure, and she stiffened against him before trying to back away from his hand. It pushed her ass into his cock, and he groaned into her ear. Her clit was hardening and swelling under his touch and he pinched it lightly, grunting with satisfaction when she moaned, and her juices flowed over his fingers.

"I hate you," she muttered.

"Aye, I can feel how much you hate me." He slid his finger easily inside of her.

"Ohhh," she sighed. Her pelvis thrust upward, and her bound hands squeezed the saddle horn. He slid his finger out and then added a second, pushing both of them inside her velvety core. Her pussy was very wet now, it sucked eagerly at his fingers, and he curled them inside of her and rubbed the front of her pussy wall with the tips of his fingers.

"Oh my God!" she cried. Her wet walls clamped down around his fingers, trapping them inside of her and he groaned with delight at the thought of her doing that to his cock later. He pressed again and her entire body trembled against him.

"Does that feel good, Elena?" he whispered into her ear.

"No!"

He nipped her neck. "Do not lie to me. Do you like having my fingers in your pussy?" He licked her neck, soothing his earlier nip.

"Yes," she moaned, and he rewarded her honesty by rubbing her clit roughly with his thumb.

She moaned again, letting her head fall back on his shoulder and panting as he circled and rubbed her clit. She was growing close, he could see it in the way she was turning her head back and forth on his shoulder, in the way she was rubbing her lower body frantically against his hand, and he stopped touching her.

She cried out in frustration. "My lord, please."

"Do you belong to another?"

She didn't answer and he brushed her clit with the tip of his thumb while he pushed his fingers deeper inside of her. She gasped and jerked against him.

"You said you have a man. Do you?"

"Please touch me," she whispered, and it took all of his willpower not to immediately do as she asked.

"Tell me the truth. Is there another who touches you the way I am touching you now?" He rubbed her wet and swollen lips without touching the small pink nub nestled between them.

"No," she gasped, "there is no other – only you."

"Good." He licked her mouth and she opened it immediately, sliding her tongue between his lips and exploring his mouth with frenzied abandonment.

He moved his fingers in and out of her as he stroked her hard clit. He kept his mouth firmly planted on hers and swallowed her loud cry of pleasure when she suddenly stiffened and arched her back. She collapsed against him as wetness flooded his fingers.

Spooked by her squirming, his horse tried to break into a trot. He tore his mouth away from hers and tugged on the reins with his free hand, returning the horse to a slow walk. He pulled his hand out from under her skirt and slipped his index finger into her mouth.

"Suck."

She closed her mouth obediently around his finger, her small tongue licking and sucking it clean. He shuddered against her, his cock throbbing in his pants. He pulled his finger free of her mouth and sucked on his second finger. He tasted her on his tongue, groaning at her good, clean taste as she attempted to sit up.

He pulled her back and cupped one bare breast, her nipple

a hard, little pearl against his palm, before he clucked to his horse. It quickened its pace and he kept his hand firmly around her breast as he searched the growing darkness.

After only ten minutes, he directed the beast to the left, leaning forward and squinting through the trees. The caves were where he remembered, and he pulled his horse to a stop. He sat and stared thoughtfully at the closest cave. She squirmed against him and he squeezed her breast once more before lacing up her shirt. He slid from the horse, leaving her tied to the saddle and, moving cautiously and quietly, entered the cave.

It was empty and he moved to the next cave. It was also empty, and he gave a grunt of satisfaction before returning to his horse. He unpacked his supplies, moving them quickly into the smaller cave as Elena sat silently on the horse. The sun had disappeared completely now, and she was shivering with the cold. He untied her hands and pulled her from the horse.

He brushed her hair back from her face and tilted her head up. He kissed her firmly, pushing his tongue past her cold lips. He cupped her ass through her skirt, squeezing it and pushing her up against his erection. He kissed her until she was trembling and leaning against him, her hands clutching the front of his shirt. He released her mouth and smiled down at her, kissing the tip of her nose as she frowned at him and tried to pull free.

He wrapped his fingers around her wrist and made her walk beside him as he led the horse to the entrance of the second cave to block the wind. He removed the saddle and, using the soft rope in his saddlebag, hobbled the horse. Between the hobbles and the large patch of dying grass the horse cropped contently, he knew the beast wouldn't go far.

He led Elena into the smaller cave and pushed her into a

sitting position. He released her wrist and grasped her chin, frowning a little at the large bruise that was forming on her cheek. "You will sit here and not move unless I tell you. Do you understand me?"

She nodded sullenly, rubbing at the red marks around her wrists as he removed his cloak and moved to his pack of supplies. He had a small lantern with him, and he lit it quickly, the cave glowing eerily in the dim light. She was shivering and she tucked her knees against her chest, wrapping her arms around her legs and burying her face in her knees. Her long dark hair was coming loose from its braid and he could see goose bumps on the back of her neck.

It was cold in the cave, even he was starting to feel the sting of the cold air. He thought about starting a fire and dismissed it almost immediately. He wanted her to be cold, wanted her to depend on his body to keep her warm, and so he pulled a thicker shirt from his pack and shrugged into it. She looked up and glared at him.

"I do not suppose you have another of those."

He shook his head, "Sorry, I do not. Perhaps you should have dressed warmer."

"I had warmer clothes in my pack," she snapped. "They were left behind when I was running for my life."

He didn't respond, bringing out some dried meat and fruit and a canister of water from his smaller pack. He sat down beside her, and she stared hungrily at the food, her stomach growling.

Without speaking, he handed her a piece of the meat. She took it from him gingerly and bit into it, closing her eyes with pleasure as she chewed and swallowed the tough meat. He ate his own piece before taking a swallow of water and then handing the canister to her. She drank, and he watched as she licked the water from her lower lip. He bit into some dried

18

fruit, chewing slowly as he stared at her. She glanced down at the fruit in his hand and he grinned and held it up.

"Would you like some fruit, Elena?"

"Yes."

He held it closer but when she reached for it, he pulled it away from her questing fingers. She snorted with frustration and he grinned again.

"Open up."

"I can feed myself." She glared at him.

"Open," he repeated.

Sighing heavily, she parted her lips and he put the fruit into her mouth, letting his fingers rest against her tongue.

She kept her mouth open and he said with a small grin, "You know what I want, Elena."

She stared at him angrily and his grin widened. "I can do this all night."

She closed her lips around his fingers, sucking on them as he pulled them slowly from her mouth. His cock, which had finally softened, immediately hardened again. He groaned softly as he watched her full pink lips pull at his fingers.

AS SHE CHEWED THE DRIED FRUIT, ELENA IGNORED THE aching in her pelvis. She would cut her own tongue out before she admitted how turned on it made her to have his fingers in her mouth. She would chop off her arm before she acknowledged that earlier he had given her the best orgasm of her life, and she would die before she confessed that when he had his fingers inside of her, she'd had to bite back her pleas for him to fuck her.

She swallowed the fruit, silently accepting the canister of water and taking another drink before he held a piece of dried meat in front of her. This time she didn't argue, just opened her mouth and took the meat, tucking it into her cheek with her tongue before sucking firmly on his fingers. She could taste the salt of the meat on the pads of his fingers, and faintly, the taste of her own body as he made another soft groan of pleasure deep in his throat.

He rubbed the pad of his finger against her tongue, his nostrils flaring as she sucked harder in response. He pulled them from her mouth, and she chewed and swallowed the dried meat as he grabbed the canister of water. He held it to her mouth and tipped it up, watching as she drank. Water started to spill out of her mouth, and he pulled the canister away and dipped his head, licking the cold drops of water from her mouth and chin. She shivered at the feel of his warm wet tongue and opened her mouth eagerly.

Instead of kissing her, he pulled back and cupped her breast through her shirt, grinning in a smug way at the feel of her hard nipple. She pulled away from him, crossing her arms over her chest and glaring at him. "It is because I am cold."

"Of course, it is, Elena."

She bristled. "Do you not know how to build a fire, my lord? Perhaps I should do it?"

He laughed and refused to be goaded by her. "It is too late to start a fire. We will be going to bed soon."

She pulled herself further away from him. "I am not sharing your bed."

"Suit yourself."

He rose and pulled a bedroll and two blankets from the larger pack. He spread the bedroll out next to the saddle and kicked his boots off, stretching out and staring at her. "Do not leave the cave, Elena. It is not wise for a woman to be alone, whether walking or," he paused and glanced at the saddle, "riding on a stolen horse. Do you understand me? You are safer here with me."

"You do not strike me as the safe option, my lord." Her entire body shook with the cold.

"Last chance to join me." He arched his eyebrow at her.

"I would rather freeze to death than join you in your bed."

"I doubt it will be cold enough for you to freeze to death, but I think you'll change your mind after a few hours."

"I will not," she insisted.

He ignored her and spread both blankets over his prone body.

"You could give me one of your blankets, my lord," she snapped. "It would seem the gentlemanly thing to do."

"True," he acknowledged. "But you must realize by now that I am not a gentleman."

He rolled onto his side, blowing out the lantern as she eyed a large rock that was just within reaching distance. She was considering bashing him over the head with it when his voice floated out of the darkness.

"I am a very light sleeper, Elena. I would suggest you do not try anything foolish."

She sighed and curled up into a tight ball, trying to warm her already freezing body. It would be a long night.

———

HE WOKE THE MOMENT SHE SHIFTED CLOSER, BUT HE KEPT HIS body still and waited to see what she would do. He'd been asleep for at least a couple of hours and he frowned, trying to identify the clicking noise in the cave. After a moment he realized it was her teeth chattering as she crawled under the blankets and flattened herself against his broad back.

"I knew you would change your mind," he said.

"Be quiet," she retorted. "I really, really hate you."

He turned over quickly and she immediately began to slide out from under the blankets, but he already had his arm around her waist and was hauling her against him.

"You are freezing," he whispered into her throat.

"I know," she chattered grumpily before resting her cold feet on his legs.

"Let me see if I can warm you up." He cupped her breast through her shirt, and she pushed his hand away.

"I did not join you in your bed for this."

He laughed. "If a woman joins me in my bed, it is for one thing only."

"Please, my lord, I am tired and cold. I want to sleep."

He hesitated and almost gave in to her quiet plea. He shook his head and kissed her neck, "Sorry, Elena. Women are not invited into my bed to sleep – only to fuck."

He nipped her throat. "Besides, fucking will warm you up much faster than just sleeping will."

He rolled her onto her back, his fingers tracing the lacings of her shirt. "Let me warm you."

"Will you force me?" she asked quietly.

He kissed the bruise on her cheek. "Never, sweet Elena. I will only take what you freely give."

The darkness of the cave prevented him from seeing her face clearly. He waited patiently, his fingers now tracing her collarbone.

"I do not know you," she said. "It is wrong to sleep with you."

"Why?" He leaned down and pressed a kiss in the hollow of her throat. "You want me and I," he pressed another kiss against her throat, "want you. Why not have what we both want? Life is too fleeting to deny ourselves."

Her soft hand touched his face and when she traced the

scar that marred it, he tried not to flinch. "How many times did you almost die in the war, my lord?"

"Many," he said shortly. "I do not wish to talk, only fuck."

There was silence. He had just resigned himself to lying next to her all night without slaking his need – despite what he told her, he would not push her out of his bed and into the cold air – when her soft fingers touched his mouth.

Her low voice drifted out of the darkness. "I want to-to fuck as well."

"Good," he whispered. He bent his head and kissed her, his warm tongue shoving between her cold lips as he unlaced her shirt and pulled it open.

He cupped her breasts, then pushed them together and ran his tongue over both nipples. They were tight and hard, and she moaned when he sucked roughly, first on the right one, and then on the left. Her back arched and her hands sunk deep into his hair, holding his head as he pulled and sucked on her nipples.

He sat up and took off both his shirts. The cold air nipped at his bare back, but he ignored it as he quickly pulled her skirt down her legs. He couldn't see her pussy, but he was aching to feel it again and to touch the soft hair that was so foreign. He pulled her legs apart and stuck his hand between her thighs. She cried out and sat up.

He was moving quickly, perhaps too quickly, but he was hanging on to his control by a thread. It was years since he'd been with a woman, and he was frantic with need for her. He cupped her pussy firmly with one hand and used his other hand to pull up the hem of her shirt.

"I want this off," he demanded.

She took it off without speaking, and he pushed her back

down onto the bedroll as she clamped her thighs around his hand.

"Open your legs, Elena," he growled.

She hesitated and then parted her legs a little. He bent his head and sucked on her nipple again. She cried out with pleasure, her fingers digging into his broad back. He lifted his head and kissed her hard.

"Wider, Elena. I want you to spread your legs wide for me," he whispered against her lips. She moaned into his mouth and spread her legs obediently. Her pussy lips parted, exposing her wet and swollen clit and he rubbed it roughly.

"Good girl," he murmured as she thrust her pelvis against his fingers.

He slipped his tongue into her mouth, and she sucked on it eagerly. Her hands moved to his chest and she touched the rough hair. Her fingernails grazed one flat nipple and he groaned before reaching to undo his pants. He pulled his cock free, took her hand and guided it to his throbbing dick.

"Touch me, Elena," he demanded.

She wrapped her fingers around the thick shaft, and he could hear her sharp inhale. She ran her hand up and down his cock and then let go and tried to squirm away from him.

"No. No way," she said. "It is too big."

He sighed with irritation and pulled her back to him. He pushed one hard thigh between hers before she could close them completely. "I will go slowly."

She shook her head. "It will not fit inside of me, my lord."

"I assure you it will."

"No, it will not," she argued.

He kissed her again, running his tongue over every inch of her warm mouth until her pelvis was thrusting against him helplessly. He put his hand against her pussy and rubbed lightly.

"Elena, I have been with women who did not become as wet as you, and they were able to take nearly all of me inside of them."

He could almost feel the heat of her embarrassment at his words. "My lord, I -"

"Feel how wet you are, sweet Elena," he whispered, his fingers gliding easily over and between the wet and swollen lips of her pussy. He slid two fingers deep inside of her and she cried out, her legs falling open.

"Your pussy is practically begging for my cock." He sucked on her lower lip. "I promise I will go slowly." He rose to his knees, slipping his pants down and pulling them off, keeping his body between her legs so she couldn't close her thighs. He braced himself on his hands above her and pressed the head of his cock against her pussy. She tensed immediately, and he rubbed her clit with the head of his dick.

"Oh, oh, oh," she repeated breathlessly. Her hands gripped his forearms tightly, her nails digging into his skin as he brought her closer and closer to climax. His cock was coated in her juices, and he placed it at her tight opening as he moved his fingers to her clit and rubbed firmly.

With a harsh cry she arched upwards, sheathing nearly half of him inside of her as she climaxed hard around him. He groaned and threw his head back as her muscles squeezed his cock. He hadn't fucked a woman in over two years and just being inside of her warm core was bringing him dangerously close.

He panted harshly as she shook and shuddered around him before collapsing on his bedroll. He took her thighs in his big, hard hands, lifting them higher and spreading them wide before pushing more of his cock into her.

She was tight, incredibly tight, but she was also warm and wet, and it took only a few seconds before his entire cock was sheathed inside of her. He propped himself up on his hands again and waited a few moments before saying, "All right?"

"A moment please, my lord," she replied.

"I cannot wait much longer, Elena," he gritted out.

"All right," she breathed.

He immediately moved within her, using long, slow strokes that made her pussy tighten around him.

He groaned, his body jerking against hers. "Stop doing that."

"I cannot help it," she moaned.

He clamped his jaw shut and increased his speed. She gave another cry of pleasure as he plunged in and out of her with hard, powerful thrusts. Their pelvises slapped against each other and she hooked her long legs around his hips as he drove into her.

He reached between them, found her clit and rubbed it. She came immediately, screaming her pleasure as her pussy contracted around him. He gave his own shout of pleasure and came inside of her, filling her with his warm seed as he shuddered above her.

He pumped in and out a few more times as her pussy pulled the last of his seed from him and then collapsed against her. She let out a soft "oof" but put her arms around him, stroking his back.

He kissed her neck and rolled off of her. Before she could protest, he turned her on her side and pulled her back against his chest as he wrapped the blankets around their naked bodies.

He kissed the curve of her shoulder, "Are you warmer, sweet Elena?"

"Hmm," she said drowsily.

He cupped one firm breast and buried his face in the back of her neck.

CHAPTER 2

Traven listened to Elena's soft moans and cries of pleasure and he smiled before kissing the side of her neck again. He had fucked her twice more, waking her in the middle of the night and then again just before they had eaten breakfast and packed the supplies. She had submitted willingly both times and now as she arched her back and gripped his strong thighs with her hands, he nuzzled his face into her hair.

At one point in the night he had unbraided her hair, wanting to feel it against his chest and shoulders. This morning when she had looked for the small piece of leather to braid it again, he'd hidden it in his pocket. He liked the way she looked with her dark hair down and wild about her face, and her cheeks still flushed from his lovemaking.

They'd eaten breakfast quickly before he had lifted her onto his horse and ridden toward home. After only a couple of hours he started again, cupping her breast through her shirt and teasing the nipple until it was erect.

She didn't protest, had even helped him to unlace her shirt and pull it from her body. Her skin was covered in goose bumps, but she didn't seem to feel the cold. He'd spent the last half hour plucking and pulling and teasing her nipples until they'd darkened to a deep red and were swollen and rock hard.

She leaned against him, her head digging into his shoulder, her hands braced on his thighs and her back arched to give him better access to her large breasts. She moaned when he rolled her left nipple between his thumb and forefinger. He could feel her pelvis moving back and forth as she pressed herself into the hard saddle trying to find relief for the ache between her thighs.

He turned his head and kissed her on the mouth, sliding his tongue between her lips and letting her suck eagerly on it for a moment. God, he loved a responsive woman, and she was more responsive to his touch than any other woman he'd taken to his bed.

She tore her mouth from his. "My lord," she whimpered. She tugged at the hand that still cupped her breast and pushed it under her skirt. He rubbed his fingers across her clit. She was soaking wet and his fingers were covered in her sweet cream in a matter of seconds. He smiled his approval and then bit the top of her shoulder as he pinched her clit gently in the way he had quickly discovered she liked.

She shuddered and bucked her hips upward, and his horse snorted nervously beneath them. He had only meant to make her come again but after watching her reaction to his touch, and feeling how wet she was for him, he had an undeniable urge to fuck her again.

They were passing a fallen tree and he pulled the horse to a stop beside it. He continued to rub her clit, watching her body and face until he knew she was about to climax and then stopped abruptly.

"No," she cried and hit his arm with frustration when he pulled it free from the folds of her skirt.

The sky had been growing progressively darker and as large flakes of snow started to fall, he dismounted quickly and pulled her down off the horse. He tugged her skirt down around her hips until it pooled at her feet and he lifted her out of it. He set her on her feet next to the fallen tree, staring down at her. Standing naked among the trees with the snow melting on her skin, her hair flowing down her back and her face flushed with desire, she looked like an exotic wood faerie. His cock was throbbing against his pants and he groaned and turned her around before pushing her roughly against the fallen tree.

She bent over it, bracing her hands on the moss-covered bark. Although he knew she must be sore, had seen it in the small grimace she made when he lifted her onto the horse this morning, she spread her legs eagerly, staring at him over her shoulder.

"My lord, please," she begged.

He stepped forward, nestling his muscular thighs between her smooth ones and forcing them even wider. He undid his pants and pulled his cock free, placing it at her wet entrance. He stared down at her pale ass before rubbing and kneading the firm flesh. She moaned and pushed back against him, taking as much of his hard cock into her as she could.

He leaned down and kissed her lower back, tracing her spine with his warm tongue.

"Patience, sweet Elena," he murmured.

"No," she muttered. "Fuck me."

Her words sent a wave of desire through his gut and he pushed into her with one hard thrust, burying himself to the hilt in her warm pussy.

She moaned again, writhing under him as he plunged in

and out of her. He reached down and grabbed her upper arms, pulling her upward. Impaled on his hard cock, her thighs spread wide and her arms held tightly in his large hands, she was helpless to do anything but shudder and gasp with pleasure as he fucked her hard and fast.

Her breasts bounced with every thrust and she threw her head back, her long hair tickling his flat stomach as she stared up at the sky, snowflakes melting on her tongue as her breath plumed out like smoke in the cold air.

The air was cold around him, but her pussy was delightfully warm and sucking eagerly at his cock. Her tight wet heat was driving him crazy. He squeezed her arms and thrust in and out of her as her pussy clamped down around him and her entire body shook with her climax. He followed quickly, pumping furiously into her as he came, his head thrown back and the cords standing out in his neck.

She started to shake with cold almost the moment he pulled out of her. He helped her dress and then made her put on his thick shirt over hers. Her lips were turning blue and he cursed himself for stripping her naked in the cold air.

He lifted her onto the horse, she made a soft whimper of pain when her legs stretched around the beast's body, and he swung into the saddle behind her. He pulled a worn and battered wide-brimmed hat from his saddle bag and jammed it down on his head before turning the collar of his cloak up. He unbuttoned it, pulled her shivering body back against him and buttoned the cloak around the both of them.

She pressed her head against his shoulder, burying her face in his neck. The wide brim of his hat protected her face from the falling snow, and she sighed softly before shifting her lower body. There was another soft groan of pain.

"Sore?" he asked.

"A little."

He reached down and rubbed her inner thighs through her skirt. "When we get home, we will have a hot bath. It will help with the soreness and to warm you."

JUST THE TOUCH OF THE STRANGER'S HAND ON HER INNER thighs, heated her up again. Elena closed her eyes and tried not to picture being with him in a tub full of steaming hot water. That was too dangerous to consider. She had no intention of going anywhere near him once they reached the safety of Lord Enderson's estate. It was one thing to go temporarily insane and allow a complete stranger to fuck her multiple times, but another thing entirely to participate in the manner that she did. The rational part of her mind was justifying it with the thought that she'd really had no choice. He might have saved her from being raped and murdered, but that didn't make him an honourable man. He was her only way to get home safely and if that meant she had to lie on her back and spread her legs for him, so be it.

But did you have to enjoy it so enthusiastically? Did you have to be quite so willing and eager? For God's sake, he just stripped you naked and fucked you over a tree in the middle of a snowstorm. And you begged him for it!

She blocked out her inner voice. It had been a long time since she'd been with a man and she couldn't be faulted for acting like a cat in heat. She may not have found him particularly attractive, not with the long hair and that bushy beard, but his mouth and his fingers were very good at coaxing the pleasure from her body and he was gentle and patient with her.

And his cock! A shiver of need went through her and mistaking it for cold, he pressed her more firmly against him.

She could feel yet another wave of desire starting in her belly and she bit her lip, cursing herself in her head.

She'd been afraid at first. She'd been afraid of the size and the thickness of him and believed without a doubt that she would not be able to take him inside of her. He had shown her differently and now she was ashamed to admit that she was actually craving his cock. The way it filled her so fully, the way it gave her pussy no choice but to stretch and accept the hard length of him, turned her on in a way she'd never felt before.

When he'd woken her in the night by placing that thick hard shaft between her ass cheeks, she became wet before she was even fully awake. His questing, probing fingers had quickly discovered just how soaking wet she was.

He'd growled his approval of her wetness, pulling her leg back and over his hip so he could enter her from behind. As she listened to the wet sounds of her pussy eagerly accepting his hard cock she'd groaned with shame, but the noisy sound of their joining seemed to increase his desire for her. He had immediately sped up, pounding his cock into her, his beard scratching her back and his hand reaching around to pinch her clit with gentle fingers.

She had climaxed immediately, a little embarrassed at how quickly and easily he had discovered the fastest way to make her come. He had taken his time in fucking her, using his rough hands to explore every inch of her creamy skin in the darkness while he moved in and out of her. She had come twice more, shaking and shuddering helplessly around his thick cock, before he finally allowed himself to come.

She was sore in the morning. Her pelvis and thigh muscles ached in a way that they hadn't for a very long time. She had come back to the cave after relieving herself to find him lying on his bedroll, one large hand stroking his erection and the other beckoning for her to join him. It was the first time she had actually seen his cock. The morning light was dim in the cave but there was more than enough light to see his cock as he pulled and stroked it.

Instead of being afraid, she had gushed wetness in response and joined him on the bedroll. He rolled her onto her back, pushed her skirt up around her waist, and while she appreciated that he slid his hand between her legs to make sure she was ready for him, it hadn't been necessary. The smug smile on his face as he entered her with one smooth thrust, assured her he hadn't failed to notice her immediate arousal. She had quivered and shook shamelessly beneath him, crying out and urging him to move faster, her cries echoing in the small cave as he coaxed another two orgasms from her body.

She'd thought she was done then, that her body couldn't handle anymore of the intense pleasure, but when he began to fondle and cup her breasts as they were riding, the now-familiar ache had started in her belly immediately.

It wasn't her fault, she decided irritably as she trembled with a combination of cold and desire. Despite his rough appearance, he was obviously a skilled lover and it had been a very long time since a man had touched her. Any woman in her position would have done the same.

As if he was reading her mind, he shifted her closer and asked, "When was the last time you were with a man?"

She remained silent and he squeezed her waist. "You will tell me what I want to know, sweet Elena."

"And if I refuse?"

He laughed, the sound vibrating from his chest and into her back. "I swear, I think you are being deliberately difficult in the hopes that I will fuck you again."

She snorted. "That loosens my legs, not my tongue, my lord."

He laughed again and moved his hand to cup her pussy through her skirt with warm familiarity. "I imagine I could get you to tell me anything while I was fucking you. You do seem to do a lot of begging when I am between your legs."

She flushed with embarrassment and tried to yank his hand away. He responded by cupping her more firmly and although there was nothing overtly sexual in his touch, she cursed inwardly at the thrill of pleasure in her belly.

"Tell me how long it has been," he said.

"A long time," she replied.

"Aye, for me as well." He shifted her closer yet, his hand still between her thighs and dropped a gentle kiss on the bruise on her cheek.

"Perhaps that is why we cannot get enough of each other," he mused.

He rubbed her gently and she placed a hand on top of his. "My lord, I am cold and sore."

"Aye, I realize that. I am not so cruel that I would ask you to pleasure me again in the middle of a snowstorm. Once was enough." There was a hint of laughter in his voice. "Besides, we are nearly home. A hot bath beckons us both, and afterwards, I will rub some healing oil into your thighs. Would you like that, sweet Elena?"

Before she could respond he studied her face and neck. "And maybe on your cheek and your neck as well."

She frowned. "What is wrong with my neck?"

He grinned at her. "I am afraid I was too rough. There are marks from my mouth and teeth on your soft skin."

She looked at him in horror. "Please tell me you jest."

He shook his head and she closed her eyes, groaning as the memory of him biting and sucking on her neck and shoulders returned to her. At the time she had found it incredibly erotic, but now she was horrified that others would see the marks.

He laughed and nuzzled her neck. "It is fine, Elena. You are not the first woman to bear the marks of her man's lust for her. Besides, the collar I will give you to wear will be more than adequate to cover the marks until they heal."

She stiffened against him. "My lord, I do not belong to you. I will not wear your collar."

His hand tightened between her legs. "You will wear it, Elena."

"No, I will not," she replied. They were only a few miles from Lord Enderson's estate, and even if he decided to dump her from his horse, it would be easy enough for her to walk the rest of the way. Even with the thick blanket of snow that was falling.

He moved his hand up her body, resting his large hand against her upper chest and stroking his thumb against her rapidly beating pulse.

"I could make you wear it," he whispered silkily.

"Aye, I suppose you could try," she responded. "But we both know that the Lord Enderson does not allow any man who lives on his land to force a woman into wearing a collar."

"War can change a man," he grunted.

"Perhaps. But until Lord Enderson returns and announces his change of heart, or you can convince him to force me into wearing your collar, you will have to find another woman to wear it."

"Women have begged to wear my collar," he said.

He sounded like a frustrated little boy and she pressed her lips together to keep from smiling. She knew why he was frustrated. Her reaction to him, the obvious enjoyment she took from his touch had made him assume she would be more than willing to accept him as her man, at least for a while.

"You were more than eager enough to fuck me earlier," he said.

"Aye, but earlier we were in the middle of the woods and I had no way to return home."

He gaped at her. "Are you telling me you fucked me as a way to secure a ride home?"

"Does that offend you, my lord?"

"I am surprised that you used me in such a manner."

She laughed. "You used me to satisfy your need, yet you are offended that I used you in order to return safely to my home? I have no doubt that if I had refused your advances, you would have dumped me in the woods and left me to freeze to death."

"I would not have," he said angrily. "Besides, you seemed to enjoy my touch."

"Aye, it was pleasant enough," she said. "But it does not mean that I wish to continue with it."

"Pleasant enough?"

She glanced at him. She was certain that he was not a man who often found himself at a loss for words. "Have I hurt your feelings, my lord?"

"No," he muttered.

She patted his arm. "I have. You said yourself that you are used to women falling into your bed and begging for the chance to wear your collar."

She patted his arm again. "Do not be discouraged, my lord. There was bound to be one sooner or later who would find you only average in bed. It happens to all men."

He grunted angrily and dug his heels into the horse's sides. The horse broke into a brisk trot and her breath hissed between her teeth as she bounced helplessly on the hard saddle. She grabbed the saddle horn, trying to stop her sore pelvis and legs from slamming against the saddle. She refused to ask him to slow down. He was obviously angry with her and doing this on purpose.

She clamped her jaw shut against the whimpers that wanted to escape. She had pushed him too far, but she wanted him to be angry with her. She did not know him well, but she knew without a doubt that he would not force himself on her. It was not him she didn't trust but herself. She had never considered herself weak-willed but there was something about him, about his voice, and his mouth, and his hands that she couldn't seem to resist. If he made any sort of advances towards her, she had no doubt that her body would betray her quickly and she would be in his bed, legs spread wide and his collar around her neck, before her brain knew what was happening.

Keeping him angry with her would dampen his desire for her, at least for a few days. The Lord Enderson's castle was large. She could easily avoid him until he found another woman to pleasure him. Her stomach twisted a little at the thought of another in his bed and she rolled her eyes with irritation.

She hissed again as she was jolted forward, and the saddle horn jabbed into her crotch. She blinked back the sudden tears.

"Sorry," he muttered. It almost sounded like guilt in his voice. He put his arm around her ribcage and pulled her body back against his. He held her firmly so that she didn't bounce, and she couldn't help her soft sigh of relief.

Neither of them spoke again until they rode over a small hill and Lord Enderson's castle could be seen.

Without looking at him, she said, "You must be happy to see your home again, my lord."

"Aye," he grunted.

As they approached the large stone wall that surrounded the estate, Elena unbuttoned the cloak and leaned forward. He stopped the horse in front of the gate and a small metal panel high on the gate slid open and a voice drifted out.

"Elena? Where are Brody and Roy? Who is that man with you?"

"We were attacked, Jameson. Brody and Roy were killed, and I would have died as well if it had not been for him. He is one of Lord Enderson's men."

"Hold on," Jameson said before sliding the metal panel closed. After only a few moments, the heavy gate opened slowly, and Elena gripped the saddle horn when he nudged his horse forward.

The stranger immediately rode for the castle and Elena twisted around to shout, "Thank you Jameson!"

He rode past the stables and stopped in front of the large grey castle. It loomed over them and as the door opened, he slid from the horse and, hooking his hands into her armpits, lifted her down from the horse. He held her for a moment, his thumbs stroking the sides of her breasts as he scanned her face.

He hesitated and then leaned down, his beard and warm breath tickling her ear. "Last chance, sweet Elena. Warm my bed, pleasure me with your body and in return I will keep you safe. No man will even dare look at you if you bear my collar around your neck."

She shook her head. "This is my home and I have nothing to fear here. I do not need your protection."

He grunted in frustration and nearly shoved her away as a blonde woman, her face wide and homely, hurried to Elena.

"Elena!" She ran her thumb over the bruise on her cheek. "What happened? Are you all right?"

"I am fine, Aldina." She smiled at the woman and hugged her hard.

"Elena?" A man, he was tall with green coloured eyes, long dark hair tied back in a low ponytail, and a kind face, approached. He gripped her chin and studied the bruise on her face. "How did this happen?"

"We were attacked, Duncan," she said.

"Brody and Roy?"

"They are dead. I am sorry. I know they were your friends."

He muttered a curse before rubbing at his ribs. "How did you survive?"

"One of Lord Enderson's men, returning from the war, stumbled upon us. He saved me and provided me with safe passage back home."

He frowned. "One of his men?"

"Aye." She tipped her chin in the stranger's direction and Duncan turned to study him.

The stranger, standing silently beside his horse, swept his hat from his head. Duncan stared at him for a long moment.

"It has been a long time, Duncan," the stranger said.

"Aye, my lord – too long," Duncan replied.

Elena watched in surprise as Duncan ran forward and embraced the stranger. He laughed and pounded him on the back, making the stranger wince.

"Easy, Duncan. I have been riding for many days and for someone who was nearly dead the last time I saw him, you are surprisingly strong."

Duncan laughed again. More people had gathered around and Duncan, clasping the stranger's arm, turned to them. "Do you not recognize your own master, you lazy sods! Lord Enderson has returned from the war!"

There was a collective gasp of surprise, and then a few

people bowed before surging forward to clap him on the back, and to grab his hand and shake it.

"Come, lord Traven. You must be tired and cold. You will rest tonight and tomorrow night we will throw a party like the castle has never seen." Duncan led him toward the castle.

The stranger, no – lord Enderson – glanced over his shoulder at her. She knew she was staring at him with wide, shocked eyes and he gave her a small grin before allowing Duncan to lead him into the castle.

CHAPTER 3

"You are lucky to have survived, Elena." Aldina sat on a chair in the servant's shared bathing room and watched as Elena sunk deeper into the tub.

"Aye, I know."

Aldina rose and washed Elena's hair for her, scrubbing her scalp with vigorous movements. "Ugh, Elena, you are filthy."

She laughed. "I slept in a cave last night. What do you expect?"

"Slept, did you?" Aldina raised one eyebrow at her. "I do not believe it was just sleeping you did last night."

Elena coloured. "You speak foolishly."

Aldina laughed. "I may be married for a few years, but it does not mean I have not had my fair share of love bites."

Elena clapped her hand over her neck. In her shock at discovering that the man who saved her life was the lord Traven himself, she'd completely forgotten about the marks he left on her neck.

She groaned with embarrassment and sunk even deeper into the water as Aldina rinsed her hair.

"Why so red?" Aldina asked. "The lord Traven is a handsome man, and there are not many women who can resist him once he sets his sight on them."

Elena closed her eyes. Aldina's taste in men obviously differed greatly from hers if she thought their employer was handsome. He could be charming and had very talented... hands, but he was not attractive.

"Will you continue with him?" Aldina asked.

"No," Elena replied. "I did not know he was the lord Traven. He never gave me his name and let me assume that he was one of his men."

She grabbed the soap and washed her body. "Besides, Bonnie still wears his collar."

She wrinkled her nose a little. She had seen the short brunette wearing the lord Enderson's collar on numerous occasions over the last few years. An ugly and garish collar, it went from the bottom of her throat to nearly her chin. Although many women had expressed their jealousy over it, Elena thought it hideous with its bright coloured jewels and the ornate details inscribed into the silver.

Aldina scoffed. "The girl tends to wear his collar only when it is convenient for her. Why, not three days ago I caught her riding one of the stable boys in the barn."

Elena laughed as she scrubbed at her feet. "It does not matter to me. I have no intention of warming his bed again."

"It is probably for the best. Lord Traven is a good man, but he is not known for his loyalty to one woman. I swear I have lost track of how many women his collar has graced the neck of. He has always been a man with a healthy appetite for the opposite sex."

"Tell me," Aldina's brown eyes lit up, "is the lord Enderson's cock as big as they say it is?"

"Aldina! I will not answer such a question." Elena blushed brightly.

The older woman laughed. "I will take that as a yes."

There was a knock on the door and one of the other servants, Danielle, stuck her head in. "I have something for Elena."

Aldina crossed the room and took the package from her. "Thank you, Danielle."

She closed the door and returned to Elena, sitting on the chair next to the tub. She unwrapped the cloth-covered object, staring at the small, amber-coloured bottle curiously. There was a note tucked in the bottom of the cloth and she held it up, squinting to read the small writing.

"It is from lord Traven. He says you will know what to do with it but if you need any help in applying it, he will be glad to assist you."

She pulled out the cork and sniffed at the opening of the bottle. "It has a soothing smell. What is it, Elena?"

Elena blushed. "A healing oil I believe."

"How kind of him. It is a nasty looking bruise on your cheek."

"Aldina?"

"Hmm?" The woman had poured a little of the oil in her hand and was rubbing it into her palms.

"Does it bother you to wear your collar?"

Aldina gave her a shocked look, her fingers stroking the leather and silk collar around her neck. "Of course not. It is a gift from my husband, my favourite one."

"You do not feel like it makes you nothing more than his property?"

Aldina laughed, "No, Elena. The collar does not make me his property. It tells the world that I am his love and he is mine. I wear it proudly."

When Elena only stared at her, her grey eyes grave, Aldina said, "I always thought it strange that your husband did not ask you to wear a collar."

"I wore a ring." Elena stared down at her bare left finger.

"Aye, and so do I. The collar is no different than the ring."

"It is," she insisted. "When a man gives a woman a ring, it is because he wants to bind himself to her for life. A collar means only that she is warming his bed and no other man may touch her."

"Aye, you have a point. But there are many marriages where the woman is nothing more than a bed warmer. What is the difference then?" Aldina asked.

When Elena didn't reply, Aldina stood and grabbed a towel. "Come, the water is cooling."

TRAVEN SIGHED AND STRETCHED HIS LONG LEGS OUT. HE HAD slept like the dead last night, perhaps it was the novelty of sleeping in a bed after so many years. This morning after touring his estate, he had taken lunch in his private chambers, inviting Duncan to join him.

He studied his friend, noting the way Duncan rubbed at his ribs. "How is your side?"

Duncan shrugged and drank some mead. "Pains me in the cold weather, but I know how lucky I am. If it had not been for your quick thinking…"

He studied Traven. "I owe you my life, Traven."

"You would have done the same for me," Traven said.

"Why did you send me home rather than keep me to continue fighting the war once I'd healed?" Duncan asked.

"Honestly?" Traven said. "I was not certain you would

live. I thought it best to send you home to die, so you could be buried next to your parents."

Duncan nodded. "Aye, I thought so. Once I healed, I had plans to return to the fight, but then…"

"Then, what?" Traven asked.

"I felt that my presence was needed here more than at the war.

Traven took a long swallow of his mead and stared into the fire. "There are many men I do not recognize, Duncan."

"Aye. They were brought in by lord Barten in the last year or so. With so many men away in the war, he felt it was necessary for protection against the roaming bands of scavengers and thieves who have popped up."

"Where did he find them?"

Duncan shrugged. "I do not know. Truthfully, I am not entirely sure that some of them are any better than the thieves that have been plaguing our lands of late."

"Where is Graham? I would have expected him to be here."

"He was called away to his family home. His father was ill. We received word two days ago that his father had died and lord Barten would be returning in the next few days. I expect he will be shocked to see you here. There was a rumour that you were killed in the war."

"Aye, so I heard," Traven said.

Duncan grinned at him. "I did not believe it."

"Has Graham done well in my absence?"

Duncan hesitated, and Traven frowned. "I would have you speak the truth, Duncan."

"He has changed. The power he perceives he now has after you appointed him temporary ruler of your lands has brought out a side of him that was well-hidden."

"Are you sure of this, Duncan? What you describe is not the man I remember."

"Perhaps I am being too harsh on him. Or perhaps I am simply seeing something that is not there."

Traven shook his head, "You are smarter and more intuitive than any man I know."

"You give me too much credit, Traven."

Traven grunted in reply and stared moodily into the fire. His thoughts returned to Elena and he sighed irritably. He could not seem to get the dark-haired beauty out of his head.

He cleared his throat. "Tell me about the woman."

"What woman would that be?"

"The one I brought back with me."

"Ahh, Elena. She is a beauty, is she not?" Duncan grinned at him.

"Aye, she is pretty enough."

"Well, from what David has told me, lord Barten hired her and her husband shortly after you left for the war. Her husband was a skilled blacksmith and she was put to work in the household."

"She is married?" Traven swallowed down the immediate jealousy. She'd told him she had no man. Why had she lied?

"She was," Duncan amended. "Her husband died less than a year after they arrived here. He contracted an illness and died after only a few days."

"Were they in love?"

"Aye, very much so. David said it was a strange relationship though. She wore a ring but no collar. There was much talk about that amongst the servants."

"Who has she been with since her husband died?"

"No one."

He stared at Duncan. "No one at all?"

Duncan shook his head. "Not that I am aware of. David

said the men gave her a proper mourning period, nearly six months if I remember correctly, but the moment she stopped wearing black, they pursued her. According to David, she has rejected them all, repeatedly. The men call her the Ice Maiden now."

"The Ice Maiden?"

"Aye, because she is so cold toward their advances. There was rumour that she was so distraught over the death of her husband that she decided to enjoy the company of women instead."

Duncan stared shrewdly at him. "Although by the looks of the fresh love bites on her neck, I imagine it is nothing but a rumour."

Traven just shrugged as Duncan grinned. "Perhaps she just had her sights set higher than a common blacksmith this go around."

Traven shook his head. "She did not know who I was until you said my name. She assumed me to be one of my men."

"Why did you not correct her?"

He shrugged again. "I do not know. I suppose I wanted to see if I could still bed a woman without her knowing who I was. It has been a long time since I have been with a woman who desired me solely for myself rather than my name and my status."

Duncan didn't reply, and Traven glanced at him. "I asked her to wear my collar and she refused."

Duncan grinned. "Aye, I am not surprised by that. If she would not wear a collar for her husband, it is safe to assume she would not wear one for you. Although now that she knows who you are, perhaps she will change her mind."

"Doubtful," he grunted.

"The wee Bonnie still wears your collar."

Traven groaned. "Oh God."

"Well, she wears it when it suits her. I do not believe she has been faithful to you in your absence."

"I will have to speak with her. I did not expect her to wear my collar during my absence. If I had not left so quickly, I would have taken it back before I went to war."

After a moment, he said, "Is there anyone Elena is close to?"

"Aye. She is close to Aldina and David. She spends a fair amount of time with them in their quarters. And there is a young beggar boy, I believe his name is Bryce, that she is fond of. She saves food for him, and I think she hides him in the kitchen during the colder nights."

The two men were silent for a few moments before Duncan shifted in his chair. "I am not sure if this matters to you or not, but since you seem to be interested in Elena, you should know that lord Barten has set his sights on her."

"Has he now?" Traven said mildly.

"Aye. Although he has not spoken to me about his plans, I believe he intends to marry her. He has been quite persistent in his pursuit of her."

"And has she responded to his advances?"

"No. She is the Ice Maiden remember?" Duncan said.

Traven snorted and stared into the fire. He did not care what Duncan said, the Elena he had held in his arms was no ice maiden. She was hot passion and flaming desire, and the way she had responded to his touch had him aching to take her to his bed again.

He sighed heavily. She would not join him in his bed willingly. She told him herself that she only used him and as much as he wanted her, he would not force her into his bed.

Duncan stood and clapped him on the shoulder. "Come, Traven. The party in your honour is about to begin."

Elena lifted the tray filled with glasses of mead and walked toward the common room. The tray was heavy, and she knew that by the end of the night her arms and back would be aching. She would use some of the healing oil on them, she decided. It had worked incredibly well on her sore thighs, and even the bruise on her cheek and the marks on her neck had faded a little overnight.

She entered the common room. It was loud and crowded with people and she could see Aldina, a similar tray held in one muscular arm, handing out drinks at one of the tables. She moved towards the largest table and balancing the tray carefully on her forearm, handed out the glasses of mead.

She moved around the table, setting the glasses of mead down and avoiding the hands of the men who reached out to pat her firm ass.

"Thank you, Elena." Duncan raised his glass to her and took a large swallow. He wiped the foam from his upper lip and grinned at her.

"You are welcome, Duncan." She smiled at Duncan and set a glass in front of the man sitting next to him. She glanced briefly at him, her gaze sliding over him disinterestedly, and was about to move on when she suddenly realized who the man was.

"Thank you, Elena."

She stared, her eyes wide and her mouth open with shock. It was the lord Enderson, his voice, those light green eyes, and the scar running down his face told her it was him, but she could hardly believe it. He had cut his hair short and shaved the thick and bushy beard off, leaving just a dark shadow of stubble.

Lord, he was gorgeous, she thought weakly. He had a

strong, square jaw and high cheekbones, a straight aristocratic nose and his lips, oh God, those lips. Free from the thick hair that had surrounded them, she could now see that they were full and firm. She had a sudden image of those lips on hers and she flushed to the roots of her hair.

He was staring at her, amusement crinkling the corner of his eyes, and he leaned closer. His voice washed over her, deep and warm like spiced rum. "Hello, Elena."

She inhaled deeply, groaning when his scent filled her nose. It was purely masculine with a hint of soap and it sent a rush of pleasure straight to her groin. Her nipples tightened and throbbed deliciously as his gaze dropped to her breasts and lingered there.

"Hello, lord Traven." She managed to squeak out.

"It is good to see you again." He took a drink of the mead, and her lips parted involuntarily when he licked the foam from his upper lip.

"Aye, you as well," she whispered.

She hurried away, her heart pounding in her chest and her cheeks stained with colour. She nearly fell into the kitchen and Aldina stared at her in alarm.

"Elena, what is wrong?"

"Nothing! I just, I mean that is – never mind." She shook her head, took a few deep breaths and willed herself to get control of her emotions.

It does not matter that he is quite possibly the most beautiful man you have ever seen, she told herself fiercely. You are not to go anywhere near him, and you will most certainly not remember how it felt to have him between your legs.

Traven groaned as he watched Bonnie weave her way through the crowd of people. She was wearing his collar, and she smiled at him before sitting in his lap. She wrapped her arms around his neck and planted her mouth on his. She kissed him eagerly, her tongue probing at his lips and he pulled his head back.

She frowned a little. "Hello, my lord. It is good to see you again. I have missed you."

"Hello, Bonnie. You look well."

"Thank you, my lord." Her hand stroked his collar. "Why did you not seek me out last night?"

"I was tired from my journey."

"Aye, I imagine you were."

She looked up as Elena approached and poured more mead into Duncan's glass and then Traven's.

"Hello, Elena." She gave the brunette a brittle smile and wrapped herself tighter around Traven's large body.

"Bonnie," Elena replied. She didn't look at Traven as she slipped around the table to the next man.

Traven's gaze narrowed as he watched the man, a loud and brutish idiot who'd been boring him for hours with tales of his conquests, move his glass so that Elena had to lean over him to fill it. He looked down the bodice of her dress and slapped her hard on the ass.

She started, spilling a bit of the mead on his hand, and he gave her a large smile. "Careful, Ice Maiden or I will make you clean my hand with your pretty little tongue."

"Shut up, Farlan," she retorted. "You have had too much to drink."

He roared laughter and yanked her against him. "God, girl, what do I need to do to get you to wrap that mouth of yours around my cock?"

She pushed away from him. "Bathing would be a good start."

He glared at her. "You best watch your tongue around me, Ice Maiden. Where I come from, a woman only opens her mouth when a man tells her to speak or undoes his pants."

"From what I have heard, there is barely enough in your pants for a woman to wrap her lips around," she said sweetly.

The man next to Farlan bellowed laugher. Farlan flushed before grabbing Elena's wrist in one meaty hand. "Your mouth is going to get you into trouble, girl."

She yanked her hand free and he reached upwards to grab her breast.

Traven jumped to his feet, dumping Bonnie to the floor with a thud. He stepped over her and pulled Elena toward him before tucking her behind his back. He studied Farlan, and the man gave him an insolent grin.

"I was only playing with the girl, my lord. Everyone knows the Ice Maiden is as frigid as -"

Traven's hand shot out and wrapped around Farlan's throat. He squeezed brutally and the man's eyes bulged with fear as he clutched weakly at Traven's hand.

"Touch her again, speak to her again, and I will spill your guts on this floor with my sword. Do you understand me, you stupid goat of a man?" Traven snarled.

Farlan nodded feebly as Traven continued to squeeze. The room had quieted, but Traven barely noticed the silence as he glared furiously at the man.

"My lord," Duncan said.

"Quiet, Duncan," Traven snapped.

He could feel anger coursing through him. He was so close to killing the man. Watching him touch her, listening to him talk about her mouth around his cock, had filled him with a rage so great it was nearly insanity.

He squeezed again, watching as Farlan's face turned purple and his eyes glazed over.

A soft voice broke through the haze of anger. "My lord?"

He turned his head, studying Elena's grey eyes as she stared up at him. She pressed her body against his arm and reached up to stroke his face with her soft hand.

"Would you join me in the kitchen, my lord? I would speak to you about something important."

She traced the scar on his face with gentle fingers. "Please, lord Traven," she coaxed. His name dripped from her tongue like warm honey.

With a low grunt, he released his grip. Farlan fell off his chair and to the floor, gasping and choking. Elena was still pressed up against him, and he took her hand and stormed towards the kitchen, bringing her with him.

He banged through the door of the kitchen. "Out!" he shouted at the two women who were standing by the sink. With frightened looks at each other, they ran from the room.

"My lord, you must calm down."

"If he touches you again, I will kill him. I swear it."

Traven's voice was deceptively soft and for a moment, Elena almost rolled her eyes at what she deemed his childish jealousy. But after a closer look at him, the way his body was vibrating with anger and the wild look in his eyes made her reconsider her reaction.

"My lord, I appreciate your," she paused, "kindness in watching out for me, but Farlan was drunk. His tongue tends to run when he drinks too much, that is all." She made her voice soft and conciliatory and stroked his arm gently.

"This is why you should be wearing my collar." He glared

53

at her, refusing to be placated. "If you were wearing it, the stupid oaf would not dare to touch you – drunk or not."

"I do not need to wear it, lord Traven. You threatened to spill his guts on the floor. I do not believe he will ever come near me again." She grinned, trying to tease him into a calmer mood.

He snorted and pushed her back against the counter. He cupped his hand around her throat, rubbing his thumb over her pulse. He smiled when it quickened under his touch, and he bent his head and pressed his lips against it.

Her entire body reacted to just that light touch, shivers of pleasure moving up and down her spine, her nipples hardening, and liquid coating her pussy.

"The bruise on your cheek is better." He pressed his lips against it next.

"Aye. Thank you for the healing oil." Her voice was embarrassingly breathy.

He cupped the back of her skull, threading his fingers into her thick braid, and tugged her head back. His anger had dissipated, and his eyes had turned jade with need and want.

"You seemed surprised to see me earlier," he said.

"I did not recognize you."

"Which do you prefer - the long hair and beard or this?"

She stared at him. "This."

"Aye, many of the women do." He ran his hand across the stubble on his face. "Apparently, this creates a very pleasing sensation when my head is between your thighs."

She flushed bright red and he gave her a predatory grin. "Would you like that, sweet Elena? Would you like to have my tongue licking your pussy? You seem to find it pleasing when I pinch your clit. What do you think it would feel like to have my lips sucking on it?"

Her nipples were now hard points and her pussy was

soaked. She let her breath out harshly as he placed his mouth just above hers.

"I would be happy to show you how it feels. Just say the word and I will gladly taste you with my tongue."

"My lord, we should not -"

He stopped her with a kiss.

His kisses were different now, she thought. In the woods and in the cave, there had been a wildness about him that she had found extremely appealing. His kisses had been full of hunger and need with a heat to them that had made her body react in a purely physical way.

She had known from the moment he kissed her neck in the woods that she would be under his broad body with her legs wrapped around his waist by that very night. Although she would deny it with her dying breath, she hadn't wanted to resist. A shamefully large part of her had needed to find out just what it would be like to have the rough, dirty man with the surprisingly gentle touch, inside of her.

Now, pressing her up against the counter, his kisses were soft and coaxing. He teased her lips with his tongue but when she opened them, he didn't slide his tongue in like she expected. He continued to lick and nip at her lips, his touch as gentle and light as a feather, and she moaned in frustration. She wanted the rough man from the woods back. The one who had tied her to his saddle, ignored her protests, and touched every part of her body like she had belonged to him.

Still, it wasn't entirely unpleasant to have him touch her so delicately. As he kissed down her neck, his stubble scraping lightly against her skin, she moaned and wrapped her arms around him. Yes, a girl could definitely get used to this side of him.

He cupped her breast, rubbing her hard nipple with his

thumb as he licked her neck. "Elena," he whispered, plucking lightly at her nipple.

"Traven," she whimpered before lifting her head and placing her mouth against his throat. She licked him, tasting the heat and sweat of his body and he groaned, cupping the back of her head as she nipped her way up to his ear. She sucked his earlobe into her mouth and stroked it with her tongue, making him shudder against her.

"Sweet Elena, I want you to join me in my bed. Wear my collar - please. Would it be so terrible to belong to me? To share my bed each night? You want me, I know you do. Tell me you will wear my collar and I will take you to my bed right now. I want to make you feel good – let me."

Her head spinning and her body throbbing with desire, she opened her mouth to moan her consent. Before she could agree, the last tiny shred of her common sense screamed at her and she twisted in his arms, turning her back to him and leaning against the counter.

"Elena?" His voice was rough with frustration.

"I told you before, my lord, I will not wear your collar. Stop asking me to do so." She deliberately made her voice harsh, hoping it would make him step away from her.

It had the exact opposite effect. He growled loudly, shoving his body against hers and reaching around to cup her breasts possessively.

"You try my patience, girl," he gritted out. "I grow tired of hearing you deny my requests."

"Then stop requesting something I will never give you."

He suddenly pulled the neckline of her bodice down, baring her breasts so that he could tug on her naked nipples. She gasped as he ground his cock against her ass and nipped her earlobe. He rubbed and kneaded her breasts roughly, and she was helpless to stop her back from arching. The man who had taken her among the trees was back, and it sent a nearly painful cramp of pleasure through her pelvis.

"You will wear my collar, Elena. Even if I have to change the very rules I created in order for it to happen."

He pulled on both of her nipples again, forcing a groan of need from her throat. She grabbed his hands, holding them still, and called his bluff. "Do you expect me to believe that you are the type of man who would make a woman wear his collar against her will?"

"Am I that transparent to you?"

"Aye."

He barked out a laugh. "You barely know me and yet…"

"What?" she said.

"Nothing."

She tugged on his hands. "Besides, your collar is already around another's neck."

The kitchen door abruptly swung open. As if speaking about her had summoned her, Bonnie stalked into the kitchen followed closely by Duncan and Aldina.

Traven turned and glared at them as Elena, hidden behind his broad back, readjusted her clothing quickly. Her face red, she slipped out from behind him. She moved a few feet away and stared at the floor.

"Lord Traven," Bonnie said, her thin face turned down in a scowl, "your party guests are wondering where you are. And this one is needed to help the rest of us serve your guests." She gave Elena a steaming look of hatred before drawing close to Traven.

She placed her small hand on his forearm and smiled up at him, his collar gleaming around her throat. "Come, my lord. I will bring you more mead."

CHAPTER 4

He woke the moment she slipped into his bed. His head fuzzy from too much mead, he sighed happily when she pressed her nakedness against his broad back. Elena had chosen to join him in his bed after all.

He didn't object when she took his hand and brought it back to her warm center. He twitched at the feel of her smooth waxed skin and twisted his head to look behind him.

"Hello, my lord," Bonnie purred. She reached around his narrow waist and took his cock in her hand. "I thought you could use some company."

He sat up, pushing her hand away from him. "It is late, Bonnie."

"Aye, I know." She smiled at him and ran her hand over the collar around her neck. "I had to help clean after the party, my lord."

"You need to leave." He pushed past her and climbed out of the bed. She stared with obvious desire at his naked body before throwing back the covers and lying back on his bed. He stared disinterestedly at her nakedness, wondering what it was he had ever seen in her.

She cupped one small breast and slipped her other hand between her legs. "You do not mean that, my lord. I know it has been many months since you have been with a woman. I am more than happy to satisfy your needs."

"No, Bonnie. I am not interested. Put your clothes on and leave."

A look of hurt crossed her face and she slid out of his bed, grabbing her dress and struggling into it. "I wore your collar while you were gone, my lord. I remained faithful to you, and this is how you treat me?"

"Faithful?" He laughed. "Aye, I have heard the rumours of your faithfulness."

She flushed angrily. "Three years is a long time, my lord. I am only human, and you are not the only one with needs. I was always faithful to you in my heart."

"You shared my bed for a week before I left, Bonnie. That is hardly enough time to form a lasting connection."

"Then perhaps you need to spend more time with me," she said. "I have many skills that would please you in bed."

When he only stared at her silently, she sniffed and turned toward the door.

"Bonnie."

She stopped but refused to look at him.

"The collar, Bonnie. Leave it, please."

She turned and gave him an angry look before pulling the collar from her throat and tossing it onto the small table near the door.

"I had heard of your cruelty, my lord, but I never expected to have it directed toward me." She yanked the door open and slipped into the hallway. She slammed the door behind her, and he sat back down on the bed, burying his head in his hands.

"Hello, Elena."

Elena tensed at the familiar voice and clenched the sheets in her hands. It had been three days since she'd returned home and she was in Duncan's bedroom, gathering his bed sheets for washing. She took a deep breath before turning.

"Hello, lord Barten."

"You are a sight for tired eyes, my dear."

She smiled stiffly as he moved closer. He was shorter than her, but his stocky body was thick with ropy muscle. He was clean shaven, and his long blonde hair was pulled back and braided neatly. Out of all the men who had pursued her since her husband's death, lord Barten had been the most persistent. She groaned inwardly as he reached out and stroked her arm.

"I have been riding for many hours and I am tired and sore. I wonder if you would be kind enough to draw me a hot bath." His faded blue eyes stared intently at her.

"Of course, my lord." She went to move past him, and he pulled her to a stop, lifting his head to sniff at her neck.

"I have missed your scent, my dear."

She stared at the floor. "I was sorry to hear about your father, lord Barten."

"Thank you. I appreciate your sympathy."

He pulled her even closer and she put her hand on his chest. "My lord, I should go and draw your bath now."

"Aye, but first I would like a welcome home kiss."

She frowned. Lord Barten had never been so bold with her before and while she did not wish to offend lord Enderson's second in command, there was no way she was kissing him.

He put his hand on the back of her neck and she resisted

when he tried to pull her face to his. A fleeting look of anger crossed his face before he smiled at her. "You would deny the master of your home one small kiss?"

"Lord Enderson is the master of my home." She immediately groaned inwardly, wondering what had possessed her to poke at the man like that.

"Aye," he said, "but I am afraid there have been many rumours of our lord Enderson's death. It is a tragedy to lose someone so young, but that is what happens in war."

"I am afraid the rumours of my demise are a little premature," a dry voice said behind them.

Elena watched as Lord Barten's mouth opened in shock and he whirled around to stare at Traven standing in the doorway of Duncan's bedroom.

"Traven! You are home." He hesitated. "It is good to see you, old friend."

"Aye, it is good to see you as well, Graham."

The two men embraced briefly, and Traven clapped the older man on the back. "I am sorry for the loss of your father."

"Thank you, my lord."

"Did you just arrive home?"

"Aye. I was asking Elena to draw me a hot bath." He looked at her, "Go on, girl. I will join you in my bedroom shortly."

"Actually," Traven said, "Elena is needed in the kitchen." He took her arm and pushed her gently toward the door. "Send Bonnie to lord Barten's room to draw his bath please."

"Yes, m'lord." Without looking at either of the men, Elena left the room.

THE SMALL PEBBLE BOUNCING AGAINST THE KITCHEN WINDOW brought a grin to Elena's face. She dried her hands and stepped out the back door, wincing a little at the cold wind.

"Hello, Elena!"

"Hello, Bryce." She drew the young boy into her arms and hugged him hard before rubbing his thin arms briskly. "You are freezing. Come inside."

He followed her into the warm kitchen, watching with interest as she fixed a plate of leftovers for him.

He sat at the table and dug into the food, eating quickly and with great relish as she sat across from him and smiled at his enthusiasm. He was dirty and smelly, and his clothes were tattered, but she was delighted to see him. He finished the food in record time and leaned back in his chair, rubbing his stomach before belching loudly.

"Bryce!"

"Sorry, Elena."

"Where have you been?"

He shrugged. "Here and there. I holed up for a while behind the butcher's shop. He gave me a few hours of work in exchange for some food."

"You are too thin," she said worriedly.

He grinned at her. "The skinnier I am - the faster I run."

She frowned. "Bryce, you promised me you would not steal anymore. Have you broken that promise?"

"No," he protested. "I have not."

He looked down at the floor and she reached out and tilted his chin up. "Bryce, tell me the truth."

Shame flooded his face and he pulled free of her grip. "I stole a few apples from the market. I am sorry, Elena, I was hungry, and you were not here. That small girl, Bonnie, would not give me any of the scraps and I could not find Aldina. Do you forgive me?"

"Oh, Bryce." She squeezed his hand. "Of course, I forgive you, my love." She looked around the kitchen. "Do you need to stay here tonight? I can sneak you back in after everyone has gone to bed."

"No, I found myself a nice warm cave just a few miles from here. If you would give me a blanket, I will be warm enough."

"A cave? Bryce, even with a blanket, I am not sure it will be -"

She was interrupted by Bonnie's angry gasp. "What is that thief doing in here?"

"He is not a thief." Elena turned and glared at Bonnie who was standing in the doorway.

Bonnie sniffed in Bryce's direction. "He is stinking up the entire kitchen. You had better not think of sneaking him into the kitchen to sleep tonight, Elena. Lord Barten will not be pleased to hear you are allowing beggars and thieves to stay in his home."

"What I do is none of your business," Elena said.

Bonnie scowled at her. "You think because the Lord Enderson is enamored with you that you can do whatever you want?"

"Shut up, Bonnie," Elena said.

"Do you honestly think that if you deny him your company in his bed that it will only make him want you more? Trust me – the lord Traven will not play games. If you do not indulge his desire for you, he will simply find another. Someone who would be more than happy to please him."

"Aye, I suppose you think that someone is you?" Elena asked as Bryce listened silently. "Oh wait, I have forgotten that he has already dumped you from his bed and made you return his collar. Perhaps you were not pleasing enough?"

Bonnie's face flushed with anger and she clenched her

small hands into fists. "I suggest you treat me more respectfully, Elena. I am not someone who you want to become enemies with."

When Elena didn't reply, Bonnie glared again at her and Bryce and flounced from the kitchen.

Elena blew her breath out and gave Bryce a small smile. "Wait here, my love. I will find you a blanket."

SHE ROLLED OFF OF HIM, HER SMALL BODY SLICK WITH sweat, and curled up against his body. "It is good to have you home again, my lord."

"Aye, it is good to be home. Bonnie." Graham stroked her naked back with the tips of his fingers. They laid together in the bed for a while before he gave her a friendly poke. "You had best scamper away to your own bed, girl. If the lord Enderson catches you with me, you will have some explaining to do."

Her face darkened. "I no longer wear the lord Enderson's collar."

He laughed. "Do not take it personally, girl. No woman ever warms his bed for long."

She sat up and pouted at him. "But I was only with him for a week. If it was not for his interest in that dark-haired bitch, I would be in his bed right now."

"What woman is that?" Graham asked curiously.

She glanced at him. "Elena, my lord. Have you not heard?"

"I have only been home for one day," he said shortly. "Tell me what I want to know and be quick about it." He gave her arm a hard squeeze.

"Elena was sent on a supply run with Brody and Roy.

They were attacked and the men were killed. Lord Enderson saved Elena from being raped and brought her home safely. Since then, he has been doing everything he can to get her to wear his collar and warm his bed. She refuses. Although the marks on her neck when she returned home would suggest that she has not refused everything he has offered her."

She stared into the darkness. "She is such a stupid cow."

He squeezed her arm until she gasped with pain. "Watch your tongue, girl."

She gave him a calculating look. "Are you jealous, my lord? It is no secret that you desire her for yourself."

He dropped her arm. "I am not jealous. Elena will be mine."

She shrugged. "I am not so sure of that, my lord. You know how lord Traven is when he wants something. As far as he is concerned, she can do no wrong. I caught her tonight feeding that idiot thief in the kitchen and when I threatened to tell lord Enderson she just laughed at me. She knows she has him wrapped around her finger and she will use it to her advantage. I suppose eventually she will spread her legs for him. She will have to if she wants to keep his interest."

She gave him a hurt look. "I do not see what she has that I do not. The lord Enderson found me perfectly acceptable before she showed up."

"You desire to be back in your master's bed, do you, girl?" Graham said.

"Aye, I do."

"And for more reasons than his big cock, I gather?"

She flushed. "There is nothing wrong with wanting to better my status, my lord. I do not wish to be a servant forever."

He stared at her. "I may know of a way to harden the

girl's heart towards lord Traven on a more permanent basis. Would you be willing to help me?"

She didn't hesitate. "Aye, I would. Tell me what I need to do."

CHAPTER 5

"Elena! Come quickly. Now!" Aldina stuck her head into one of the many bedrooms in the castle and held her hand out impatiently.

Elena glanced up. She was scrubbing the floor in front of the fireplace and she rubbed at her knees as she stood. "What is wrong?"

"It is the beggar boy Bryce. Oh, there is no time! Come with me now. I will explain as we go."

"What is going on?" Elena asked as Aldina hurried down the wide hallway.

"Bryce is in the common room. He has been accused of stealing from lord Traven, and lord Barten is holding some kind of trial."

"A trial?" Elena stopped dead in her tracks. "What do you mean?"

"We must hurry, Elena," Aldina said.

Her heart thumping wildly in her chest, Elena pushed past Aldina and raced down the hall toward the common room. She burst through the doorway, staring wildly about for

Bryce. He was standing in the middle of the room, a heavy rope tied around his wrists and looking very small and afraid.

She ran across the room and put her arm around him, pulling his thin body against her. "Do not be frightened, my love."

Bryce gave her a scared look. "I swear I did not steal it, Elena."

"Steal what?" she asked.

"Your young friend here has been accused of stealing the lord Enderson's pocket watch."

She looked up to see both the lord Barten and lord Traven sitting in chairs next to the fire. Bonnie was standing beside lord Barten, a smug look on her face. Elena glanced at the crowd who had gathered in the room. Her breath caught in her throat when she saw Neilan, the farrier, leaning against the wall with a short but sharp looking hatchet in one meaty hand.

"I would know what proof you have of this," she said.

"It was found in his possession," lord Barten replied. "He was discovered eating food in the kitchen and brought to me for punishment. I was simply going to lash him a few times to teach him a lesson for stealing food, only the watch was found in his pocket."

He turned to Traven who was sitting silently. "He must be punished, my lord. I suggest that you follow common practice and have his hand removed. It will be a reminder to him and others who would try to steal from you that we will show no mercy to thieves and beggars."

"No!" Elena cried.

"Quiet your tongue!" Lord Barten snapped at her.

"Your punishment would seem too severe, Graham. He is only a boy," Traven said quietly.

"My lord, forgive me but you have been gone for a long

time. Things are not the same – the thieves and the rapists and the beggars are running rampant. They must be punished harshly if we are to restore order to your lands."

Lord Barten stared at the frightened boy. "This one has been a particularly bothersome pest. This is not the first time he has been caught stealing."

"He stole food so that he would not starve to death," Elena said.

She turned to Bryce, cupping the back of his head and bending until she was eye level with him. "Bryce, you must tell me the truth – did you steal the lord Enderson's pocket watch?"

"No, Elena, I swear." Bryce pointed with his bound hands at Bonnie. "I was standing at the back door waiting for you when that one invited me into the kitchen for food. She gave me the pocket watch. She told me it was hers and she had no more use for it."

"I did no such thing!" Bonnie cried out. "How dare you, you miserable little thief!"

"He would not lie to me," Elena said. She turned to Traven. "Please, my lord. If Bryce said he did not steal it, then he did not. I give you my word."

He stared silently at her as Lord Barten laughed. "What good is the word of a woman?" He turned to Traven. "Tell me you are not falling for her lies, my lord."

Traven studied Elena and Bryce. "Bonnie has been in my home for many years. It would not be like her to lie or steal from me."

Elena pulled Bryce closer as Lord Barten beckoned for Neilan to move forward. The farrier pushed his large body away from the wall and walked toward them, swinging the hatchet lightly in his hand.

"Not so fast, Graham," Traven said.

Graham rolled his eyes. "Traven, you must trust me in this matter. Have I not been keeping your lands and your home safe while you were gone? You said it yourself that Bonnie has been a faithful servant for many years. You cannot believe the word of a thief over hers."

He pointed to Elena. "This woman has invited and hidden the thief in your home many times. Is it no wonder that he thought he could steal from you? You should have her lashed over this."

Elena gave him a defiant look as Traven growled, "She is not to be touched."

"Fine. But we must send a message to others who would try to steal from you. You know this," lord Barten said.

Traven sighed heavily and looked at Elena. "He is right."

She gave him a look of wounded desperation and he gave her an almost guilty look before glancing away. "Do it, Neilan."

The crowd made a low muttering sound, Elena couldn't tell if it was an approving sound or not. Desperation made her back away from Neilan, Bryce wrapped securely in her arms.

The crowd's muttering increased in volume, obviously, they were surprised at her insolence. She stared at Neilan before taking a deep breath.

"My lord!" Her voice rang out steady and only a little high-pitched with nerves. "I will warm your bed tonight if you show mercy on the boy."

Lord Barten laughed and gave her a look of disbelief. "You think offering yourself will -"

"Only one night? Is the boy's hand worth just one night, Elena?" Traven's voice was low, but clear.

She didn't answer, just clutched the boy tighter to her breast.

"Wait, Neilan," Traven said.

The farrier stopped where he was, swinging the hatchet idly from hand to hand.

Lord Barten stared at Traven. "My lord, you cannot be serious about -"

Traven held his hand up, silencing him. "One month."

Elena glared at him. "Two days."

He grinned. "Two weeks."

"Three days."

"One week, and you will wear my collar for the entire week. That is my final offer. Accept it or watch the boy lose his hand."

"Agreed," she said.

Traven stood up, stretching his large body and cracking his knuckles before looking at the crowd. "The boy goes free. No one is to harm him."

"Traven, have you gone mad?" Graham snapped. "You would have a woman rule your home? The men will start to think you are weak. That you allow your dick to make -"

"Hold your tongue Graham!" Traven suddenly roared at him. Bryce flinched and hid his face against Elena's breast. She hugged him briefly before starting to unwind the heavy rope from around his wrists.

"You would be wise to not question my decisions, Graham." Traven lowered his voice. "I am grateful for your assistance while I was away, but I have returned. I will make the decisions regarding my lands. Do you understand me?"

Graham nodded and stalked away as Bonnie, a look of confusion and anger on her face, slunk after him.

"The show is over." Traven glanced at the people still in the common room. "Go on, leave."

He held his hand up as Elena started to leave with Bryce. "Not you two." He walked toward them, staring at them both as Bryce pressed closer to Elena.

"I wish to speak alone with you, boy," Traven said.

Bryce gave Elena a frightened look and she smiled encouragingly at him. "It is fine, Bryce. He will not harm you."

"Elena, you are to go to my room and wait for me there." He glanced over at Aldina. "Draw her a bath would you please, Aldina?"

"Aye, m'lord," Aldina said.

"Go to my bedroom, Elena." He gave her a look of such smoking desire that she could feel her nipples hardening in response. "I will join you shortly."

ELENA WISHED THE HOT WATER OF THE BATH WOULD CALM her. Unfortunately, it wasn't working. She glanced at the door and then at the bed, her stomach tightening with a combination of nerves and desire. Aldina had left a few minutes ago to grab a nightgown from Elena's room. As she walked back into the room, Elena stared at the nightgown she carried.

"Aldina!" she said when Aldina held up the thin piece of clothing. "Did you have to bring that one?"

Aldina ran her hand over the silky, sheer white fabric. "It was the prettiest one in your cupboard, Elena."

Elena sunk deeper into the large metal tub, closing her eyes. She had bought the garment to wear on the evening of her second wedding anniversary. Three months before their anniversary her husband had died, and she had shoved the nightdress to the back of her cupboard. She had not looked at it again.

"I am not trying to be pretty for him," she grumbled. "I do this only to save Bryce's hand."

"Aye, of course you do," Aldina said.

Elena glared at her as Aldina held up a towel. She stood and stepped into it, winding it around her body. "It is true, Aldina."

Aldina sat her down in front of the fireplace and ran a comb through her wet hair until all the tangles were gone. "There is nothing wrong with being attracted to him. You have been a widow for over two years now. I do not believe your husband would have wanted or expected you to remain alone in your bed forever."

Elena didn't reply, just stared moodily into the fire.

"Shall we braid your hair or leave it down?" Aldina asked, running her hand over the soft, damp locks.

"Braid it," Elena said immediately. She had a feeling that Traven preferred her hair down.

Aldina quickly braided her hair before Elena stood and pulled the nightdress over her head. Aldina helped her adjust it, pulling the ties at the back and lacing them tightly until the soft material hugged her breasts and skimmed her flat belly.

Aldina looked her up and down, "You look lovely, Elena. Lord Traven will be very pleased."

She hesitated, glancing at the area between Elena's thighs. Her pubic hair was a dark shadow beneath the sheer garment. "I have wax in my room. Would you like me to bring it to you? I can help you."

Elena laughed, "That is kind of you, but no thank you."

Aldina frowned. "Elena, it is custom for women to remove all of their hair."

"A man's custom," Elena snorted. "I will not rip out all of my body hair just because a man demands it."

"But the lord Traven -"

Elena gave her a wry look, "As you are well aware, the lord Traven has already seen everything I have to offer. The hair between my legs did not give him a moment's pause."

That statement was not entirely true, she mused to herself. He *had* paused, running his fingers over the hair and questioning her about it while she had trembled and waited breathlessly to see if he would continue or stop. She had been secretly thrilled when he continued.

"Elena?"

Aldina was standing in front of her. The lord Traven's collar was held loosely in one hand. They'd seen it tossed carelessly onto a small side table beside the door when they'd entered the bedroom.

Elena studied it, her face wrinkling in distaste at the gaudy jewels. As Aldina reached up to place it around her neck, she jerked back, folding her arms over her torso.

"You promised him you would wear his collar," Aldina said.

"Aye, I did. But he is not here yet and I will wear it no longer than I absolutely have to. Leave it where you found it, Aldina. I will wear it only when he insists that I do."

"All right." Aldina gave her a cheeky look. "Enjoy your evening, Elena."

She dropped the collar on the side table and gave Elena a small grin before leaving. Elena stared at the collar from across the room. Perhaps she could convince him that she did not need to wear it. She snorted loudly. That would never happen.

She paced nervously in front of the fire again. It was almost two hours since he had sent her to his bedroom, and she was beginning to wonder if he would ever show.

The door opened and Traven entered the bedroom. He kicked off his boots and pulled his shirt over his head. She swallowed thickly. It had been dark in the cave and this was the first time she had gotten a good look at him without his shirt. She stood completely still and drank in the sight of his naked torso.

He was tanned all over despite the cool weather, with broad shoulders and hard, muscular arms. His wide chest was covered in dark hair. Ridges of muscle lined his stomach and she swallowed again as her eyes followed the dark trail of hair below his navel. It disappeared into his pants and she let her gaze drop to his crotch. His erection was obvious, even through his pants, and she looked away, her heart thumping madly in her chest.

TRAVEN STARED AT ELENA. SHE WAS WEARING A WHITE nightdress and the glow of the fire behind her had turned the already sheer material translucent. He could see her high, firm breasts, their nipples already hard and waiting for his touch, the swell of her hips and - he took a deep breath - the dark shadow between her thighs.

He was suddenly aching to taste her on his tongue, to pull the flimsy garment from her body, push her legs apart and bury his face between her thighs. She was staring at a spot on the wall, her face flushed and her eyes wide with a combination of fear and excitement.

He made himself take another deep breath and look away from her. If he didn't, he was afraid he would come in his pants.

His gaze caught on the collar on the side table. He crossed the room, reached for the collar and then hesitated briefly before pulling open the drawer of the table and removing a small wooden box. He carried both it and the collar toward her.

He watched the excitement fade from her eyes as she

stared at the collar in his hands. She crossed her arms over her torso, her body stiff.

"You said you would wear it," he reminded her gently.

"Aye, I did," she said. "Where is Bryce?"

"He is fine." He draped the gaudy collar around his wrist before removing the lid from the wooden box.

She stared curiously at the object in the box. It was a leather collar, plain and unremarkable looking, with parts of it faded and worn smooth. There were no fancy jewels attached to it or ornate designs etched into its worn leather. Only his family's crest, stitched in threads of gold and blue on a small section of the leather, identified it as belonging to him.

"You may choose which collar you will wear."

"This one," she said immediately, pointing to the leather collar.

When he didn't move, she looked up at him. "What is wrong, m'lord?"

"Nothing." He draped the more ornate collar on the side of the metal tub. "Turn around."

She turned her back to him and he stood behind her, his erection brushing against her round ass. She shivered when the cool leather kissed up against her skin. He traced the back of her neck with one finger before he pulled the collar snug and buckled the small silver clasp.

"Is it too tight?"

She shook her head, and he bent his head and pressed a kiss just above the collar. He pulled the leather tie from the end of her hair and quickly unbraided it, pushing his face into the damp silken tresses and inhaling deeply. He admired the way it flowed down her back like a dark waterfall, before turning her around to face him.

He stared down at her, feeling an overwhelming urge to protect her, to make sure that all other men knew she was his.

The collar would do that – at least for the next seven days. It looked good on her, like it belonged around her neck, and he frowned at the thought that she would remove it the moment the week was up.

"You look beautiful tonight, Elena."

"Thank you, my lord." She was staring at his chest and he used gentle fingers to tip her face up towards his.

She was trembling, her eyes bright with both shame and desire, and he frowned a little, "Do not look like that, sweet Elena."

He placed a soft kiss on her mouth. "You look beautiful wearing it, like it was meant for you." He cupped her throat, rubbing his thumb along the soft leather. "It will keep you safe when you are not with me."

"Aye, my lord. But for the next seven days only."

"I remember," he said gruffly.

The shame was still in her eyes and he suddenly couldn't stand to see it there any longer. He dipped his head and kissed her, pushing his tongue possessively into her mouth and stroking hers. He kissed her repeatedly, his mouth sucking on her bottom lip, his tongue licking and darting and flicking, as he tried with his kisses to remove all the shame she felt at wearing his collar. His stubble scraped across her chin and he groaned when she pressed herself against him and kissed him back.

This time when he pulled back and looked into her eyes, there was only a dark desire in them, and he felt an answering call in his own body.

He pulled her into the circle of his arms, cupping the back of her head and shuddering when she placed wet, open-mouthed kisses against his chest and shoulders. He hissed when she bit the top of his shoulder with her small, even teeth.

79

She grinned up at him. "Revenge tastes so sweet, my lord."

"You are to call me Traven when you are in my bed," he demanded.

She leaned in to nuzzle his neck. He moaned at the feel of her warm wet tongue but when she went to bite him, he threaded his fingers in her hair and pulled her head back with a hard tug.

"Vixen," he whispered. He pulled her head back until her throat was completely exposed. His cock swelled in his pants at the sight of his collar around her neck and he pressed his erection against her. He licked her throat with agonizing slowness before capturing her mouth again.

She returned his kisses eagerly, her tongue darting into his mouth to stroke his. He groaned and kept his mouth still, letting her take charge, letting her explore and taste and tease him with her lips and tongue. She pressed herself hungrily against him, running her hands over the rippling muscles in his back, and tracing her fingers across his abdomen before sliding her fingers through the hair on his chest.

Her fingers grazed one flat nipple and he jerked and moaned into her mouth. She immediately circled back to his nipple, running her thumb over it before she pinched it between her fingers. He moaned again, his fingers digging into her waist as she bent her head and licked his nipple with her small, warm tongue.

He pushed her away, breathing harshly through his nose, and pulled at his pants in an effort to relieve some of the pressure.

"What is wrong, Traven?" she whispered teasingly. "You do not like my kisses?"

He pulled her back into his arms, his hands reaching for the ties of her nightdress. He untied them and tugged at the laces, loosening the garment. He pushed the gown from her shoulders, tugging it past her breasts and watching as it slipped down her hips and pooled at her feet.

She stepped out of it and as his eyes glittered hotly over her body, she blushed and began to raise her arms to cover herself.

"No." He pushed her arms back down to her sides. "Let me see you."

He looked her up and down, his hot gaze bringing a flush to her body. This was how he wanted her to look whenever she was in his bedroom, he decided. Naked except for his collar, her hair down and her skin flushed, with her mouth swollen from his kisses.

He stared at the collar again. God, it turned him on to see her wearing it. She belonged to him now. Every man who gazed at her would know immediately that she was his woman and to touch her would invite death. Seeing her in his collar brought out a deep primal instinct in him that seeing other women in it did not, and he was shocked to realize that for the first time in his life he wanted to please a woman in other ways than sex.

He wanted her to sleep in his bed, to sit next to him while they ate and tell him about her day. He wanted to know everything about her – where she came from, did she have brothers and sisters, did she still mourn for her husband.

"Traven?" Her soft voice washed over him, and he pushed the foreign feelings away. He had only seven days with her – he would not waste it.

"Are you all right?" she asked.

"Fine," he said hoarsely.

He dropped to his knees in front of her and kissed her abdomen. She gasped and clutched at his head as he traced her navel with his tongue and then blew on it. He nuzzled his face into the soft hair between her thighs before kissing it lightly.

"I want to taste you on my tongue, sweet Elena."

She moaned as he worked his hand between her thighs, pushing them apart. He licked the lips of her pussy and her knees buckled. She braced her hands on his shoulders giving him an almost desperate look of desire.

He grinned up at her. "The bed I think."

He rose to his feet, lifted her easily, and carried her to the bed. He laid her down on it and kissed his way down her body, his mouth lingering on her hard nipples until she was crying out and arching against him. When he was once more kneeling between her legs, his hot breath stirring her soft curls, he stared up at her.

"Open your legs, Elena. Let me taste your sweetness."

She bent her knees and let her legs fall apart. He dipped his head and licked her wet pussy. She cried out, her hands grabbing the bed sheets, and he paused. "Should I stop?"

"No," she cried breathlessly. "Please, Traven, do not stop."

He rested his hands on the inside of her thighs, pushing lightly until she was completely open to him. He stared at her small, pink clit then licked it with just the tip of his tongue. She moaned and arched her hips, pushing her pussy directly into his mouth.

He licked her clit again and again as she writhed under him. She grabbed his head in her hands, pushing and cupping his skull as he flattened his tongue and licked her with hard strokes.

ELENA THREADED HER FINGERS THROUGH TRAVEN'S DARK hair. From the moment Traven had licked her pussy, she'd lost the ability to think straight, to see straight, to even breathe properly.

"Traven, oh my God," she moaned. His dark shadow brushed deliciously against her inner thighs, sending little sparks of pleasure from her thighs down to her toes. She curled her toes into the bed and stared sightlessly up at the ceiling. Her pelvis was throbbing and aching with need and she couldn't stop panting. She wanted to beg him to stop, beg him to continue, beg him to fuck her but she couldn't do anything but grip his head and moan.

"Oh, oh God, oh..."

He pushed her pelvis down and held her still as he wrapped his lips around her clit and sucked it into his mouth.

She came immediately, crying out and shuddering against his mouth. He continued to suck on her clit until she tried to twist away from him.

"Traven, stop," she gasped out.

He slid up her body, nestling his body between her legs and kissing her throat. "Have I hurt you, sweet Elena?"

She shook her head, panting harshly, "No, m'lord. It was just very sensitive."

He smiled and kissed her mouth. She sighed and returned his kiss, tasting herself on his tongue. She wrapped her long legs around his hips, and he groaned and propped himself up on his hands above her. She stared up at him for a moment before reaching between them and grasping his cock. He groaned again at the feel of her soft hand and she stroked him back and forth for a few seconds.

"Elena," he half-moaned, half-sighed and she smiled up at him before guiding his cock to her wet opening. He slid into her wet warmth and they both cried out with pleasure.

Elena stared up at Traven's face, watching as he closed his eyes and moved slowly within her. She braced her feet on the bed and met each of his strokes. He made a low guttural noise and moved faster. His breathing was harshening, his body starting to lose its steady rhythm within her. She could feel spirals of pleasure growing in her belly, radiating down into her pelvis, and she hooked her legs back around his hips and closed her eyes. Her fingers dug into the hard biceps of his arms as she thrust her pelvis against his and searched for her own release.

He moaned her name and she opened her eyes, staring up at him as he thrust harder and harder.

"Traven," she cried out, "it feels so good, so..." she caught her breath as her orgasm rushed through her and her body arched off the bed. He groaned and buried his face in her soft throat, plunging wildly in and out until he came with a whole-body shudder. His warmth flooded her pussy and he pressed a kiss against one hard nipple before rolling off of her.

He relaxed beside her, propping himself up on one arm and staring down at her flushed and perspiring body. She started to shiver, and he pulled the covers up around them. He spooned her tight, wrapping one arm around her waist and burying his face in her neck.

He fell asleep almost instantly. Elena stared up at the ceiling. Her fingers traced the worn leather around her neck as the pleasure faded from her body. She sighed as Traven shifted closer to her, throwing one heavy leg over hers and snoring quietly.

Her body, which had been in a permanent state of arousal since she met Traven, was temporarily satiated, but her mind was in turmoil. Traven was the first man she had slept with since her husband and she was upset to realize that the guilt she always expected to feel was not there.

She'd taken off her wedding ring over a year ago, unable to stand the biting stab of loss she felt every time she saw it on her finger, and now she was wearing another man's collar around her neck. She had sworn she would never wear one, would never allow a man to own her in that manner, and would not agree to marry her husband until he accepted it.

He had wished her to wear one, she could see it in his eyes every time he looked at her, but as much as she loved him, she couldn't do it. Now, she wore the collar of a man she'd known for less than a month and she was suddenly and bitterly ashamed of herself. She refused to wear a collar for the man she had loved more than anything, but she would wear Traven's.

She could try and fool herself into believing she had done it to save Bryce's hand, but that had only been a part of it. She wanted to be in his bed, wanted to feel his arms around her, and hear his voice whisper sweetly to her. Even if it meant wearing his collar.

She blinked back hot tears. She recognized the feelings stirring within her, and she both resented and embraced them. She had thought her ability to fall in love had died with her husband and while she was happy to discover it hadn't, she was a stupid idiot for falling for someone like Traven.

He kept women only for a short time before discarding them. She knew this and she was still falling for him. Why? She barely knew the man. A big cock and an absolutely astonishing ability to make her come repeatedly was not a reason to fall in love with someone.

It was lust, she decided abruptly. Not love, only lust. It had been so long since she'd been in love that she was confusing it with lust. She'd promised him a week and she would sate her lust for him over the next seven days. Once the week was over, he would move on to someone else and she would go back to her comforting, if not lonely, routine.

Her fingers traced the embroidered crest on the smooth leather. She wondered why he had this one tucked away and wondered how many other women's necks had felt the smoothness of its leather against their skin. Had there been one who had complained of its simplicity? Was that why he had such an elaborate one created?

It didn't matter, she suddenly decided. All that mattered was she didn't have to wear that hideous sparkling collar. This one was almost pleasant to wear, its leather soft and warm against her throat, and so light that she had already forgotten it was around her neck. Perhaps it would not be so bad to wear his collar after all.

She sighed as Traven snorted softly in his sleep and tightened one thick arm around her. She was acting like a silly, love-struck fool. All those years of hating the sight of them, of flat out refusing to wear one and silently judging other women for wearing it so eagerly. And now, less than two hours after he had put it around her neck, she was already accepting it.

Seven days, she told herself bitterly. *You will wear it for seven days, you will enjoy the pleasure of his bed, and then you will remove the collar and not allow yourself to wallow in self-pity when he moves on to another.*

She stared up at the ceiling. She was tired and Traven's bed was warm and comfortable, but dinner preparations would be starting soon, and the other servants would need her help. Carefully, she lifted his arm off her and eased her way to the edge of the bed.

She stood and tiptoed across the room to retrieve her clothing from the chair that Aldina had left them on. She'd just slipped into her shirt when Traven's rough voice washed over her.

"You would leave my bed so quickly, sweet Elena?"

She cleared her throat and turned to face him. "It is nearly time to start dinner, my lord. I need to go and help the others."

He was sitting on the edge of the bed, the sheet drawn carelessly around his hips, leaving his torso and one long and lean thigh bare. She swallowed heavily at the sight of his tanned muscular skin as he ran a hand through his hair.

"You agreed to share my bed for seven days."

"Aye," she said, "I know. I will come back after dinner is finished. It is not fair to the others that they have to take on my share of the work."

He grinned at her. "How very diligent of you."

"You would make fun of me for doing my job?"

He shook his head. "No, sweet Elena, I would never do that. Come back to my bed. You are tired, I know you are."

She glared at him. "That's a very kind offer, my lord, but you told me yourself that women are invited to your bed only for fucking, not for sleeping. I was starting to get sleepy and decided I would leave your bed before you kicked me out of it."

He winced. "Elena, it is not like that."

She tugged her skirt on angrily and slipped into her shoes. "Is it not? You have made it perfectly clear what is required of me. I will wear your collar and I will join you in your bed for fucking. Those are your rules and I will follow them."

"Elena -"

"May I please leave, my lord? I will come back tonight if you wish to fuck me again," she snapped.

His face turned red with anger. "Go on then, girl. Go and do your job. I will decide later if I wish for your company or not. Perhaps I will find someone more pleasant to warm my bed this evening."

She couldn't hide the hurt that flashed across her face. A look of chagrin crossed his and it looked like he might even apologize. Before he could, she lifted her chin and stared coolly at him. "Perhaps you will."

She stomped out of his room, slamming the door behind her.

CHAPTER 6

Traven watched as Elena moved around the table, a jug of mead in one hand and a jug of water in the other. She poured them into empty glasses, avoiding the wildly flailing hands of some of the more drunk guests.

She had left his bed and he was still pissed about it. She was deliberately trying to provoke him, trying to avoid sharing his bed by making him angry with her, and he had walked right into it. He would be smarter next time and not make it so easy for her.

As she approached the head of the table, he could see her body stiffening and she avoided looking at him as she poured mead into Duncan's glass.

"Hello, Elena."

"Hello, Duncan." She smiled warmly at his best friend and sharp jealousy bit at Traven's stomach. He knew Duncan had no interest in her, but he hated that she smiled at him like that.

He almost grinned when Duncan glanced at the collar around Elena's neck and his mouth dropped open. Duncan had been in the common room when Elena made her desperate bargain with him, but no doubt, he believed that Traven would make Elena wear the other collar. Only Duncan knew the significance of the collar around Elena's throat, and Traven could see the confusion in Elena's gaze as she self-consciously touched the collar.

She moved around to his side, but he put his hand over his glass. "Water for me, girl."

He had only seven days with her, he wouldn't waste any of it by being drunk. And if she thought she'd get away with serving him dinner and pouring him drinks every night, she was sorely mistaken. He would allow it for this evening, but after tonight she would realize that her only job for the next seven days was pleasing him.

ELENA POURED WATER INTO TRAVEN'S GLASS. JUST BEING around him made her hot and needy, and dammit, where had her willpower gone? She ignored her urge to toss aside her water and mead jugs, straddle Traven and rub her pussy against him.

She moved to lord Barten, mentally preparing herself for his nasty habit of grabbing her ass while she poured his drink.

"Elena." Barten gave her a greasy grin and put his arm around her, his hand dropping below her waist. Before he could grab a handful of her ass, Traven made a sound deep in his throat. There was no anger behind it from what she could tell, but Barten immediately dropped his hand back into his own lap.

She poured the mead, unwilling to admit to herself that she was actually a little thankful for the collar around her neck. It had been like this all night. The usual pinching and groping, the ass-slapping, the rude comments made as she served the food, had completely disappeared. The men were actually respectful, saying please and thank you as she served them their dinners, and not one of them had stared at her ass or her breasts.

She wondered if it was the collar alone that made them so polite or that it was Traven's collar. The latter, she decided. It was very clear that the men had a great deal of respect for him, but she had not realized that being his woman would generate a certain courteous behavior towards her as well.

It was a nice change, she thought ruefully. She would miss it after the seven days were done.

Is that all you'll miss?

She squashed that thought down fiercely. It didn't matter anyway. She'd made him angry tonight and he would fill the empty space in his bed with another. Perhaps he would ask for his collar back as well. Anger and jealousy and a touch of hurt washed over her at the thought of him with another woman. Her hands trembled and mead splashed out of the glass. Murmuring an apology, she grabbed a rag from the pocket of her apron and wiped up the mess.

HIS ANGER SIMMERING JUST BELOW THE SURFACE, TRAVEN watched as Elena poured mead into Graham's glass. He'd managed to keep himself under control, giving only a low sound of disapproval when Graham reached for Elena's ass, but his anger was growing by leaps and bounds.

The collar she wore announced to Graham and everyone else that Elena belonged to him, and the impudent way that his second in command stared hungrily at her breasts, was a jagged knife tearing at Traven's flesh. His hands clenched into fists and only Duncan's hand on his arm stopped him from rising out of his chair and pummeling Graham into a bloody mess.

"Easy, my friend," Duncan said in a low voice. "Beating your second in command in front of everyone is not a wise move."

"Then he should keep his gaze to himself," Traven muttered.

"Aye," Duncan said, "he should. But I'm surprised he even kept his hands to himself. I told you, he wishes to claim Elena for his own."

As Elena finished pouring Graham's drink and straightened, Traven called out, "Girl!"

She turned and stared at a spot behind him. "My lord?"

"Come sit on my lap."

Her face went red and she finally looked at him. He smiled a little. Her anger with him had turned her eyes a dark and stormy grey, the exact colour they turned when he was fucking her, and his cock stirred in his pants.

She hesitated before setting the jugs on the table, and then sitting down gingerly on the edge of his knee. He yanked her back into his lap until her ass was snug against his crotch, enjoying the sound of her soft gasp.

He turned her head toward his and kissed her, slanting his mouth over hers and pushing at her lips with his tongue until with a soft groan she opened her mouth. He kissed her until her body relaxed and melted against his, until he was sure that she had forgotten about the other people at the table, until he was sure that Graham and everyone else knew she belonged to him.

Someone at the table gave a loud roar of approval, thumping their glass against the table and as the others joined in, clapping and cheering, Elena pulled her mouth from his.

Her face was bright red, and she muttered what sounded like a curse.

He grinned and stared at her for a moment. Her lips were swollen and reddened from his kisses. Her eyes were still that stormy grey colour, but now it was desire that had darkened them, not anger. He decided he preferred the desire and cupped the back of her neck, pulling her face down to him for one last kiss before he allowed her to leave his lap.

Her face red, she grabbed the jugs from the table and walked quickly out of the room.

"My lord?"

Traven turned, groaning inwardly when he saw Bonnie trailing after him. He was on his way to the kitchen to find Elena. He didn't care if she was finished work or not. He wanted her in his bed. He wanted to touch her again, to hear her soft cries of pleasure, and he was a man used to getting what he wanted.

"Hello, Bonnie." He paused, as she caught up to him and laid one small hand on his arm. He frowned at her tear-stained face. "What is it? Have you been hurt?"

"No, m'lord," she replied. "I just, I wanted to know what I did that displeased you so. Why you no longer want me?"

"You did nothing wrong, Bonnie."

"Then why, my lord? Why do you no longer want me in your bed?" she asked in a wavering voice.

"Bonnie, I," he hesitated, not wanting to hurt the young woman's feelings. "I am different now than I was before the war. It has nothing to do with you."

Now she did begin to cry, big fat tears that dripped down her pale face and darkened the front of her dress. "You lie. It is me." She pushed her way into his arms, leaning her head against his chest and sobbing loudly.

He patted her back awkwardly, wishing he could just walk away. "It is not. I promise you, Bonnie. Stop your crying." He tried not to let the irritation he felt show in his voice.

She stared up at him. "I would please you very well, lord Traven. If you would only give me the chance to prove it."

He shook his head. "No. Our time is finished."

With a soft cry, she reached up and yanked his head down, pressing her mouth against his. Shocked by her boldness, he hesitated, and she pushed her tongue between his lips. He grabbed her arms and pushed her away just as Elena appeared in the hallway. Her tanned face turned pale and her eyes filled with hurt, and he muttered a low curse.

"Elena, wait," he demanded as she turned and headed toward the servant quarters.

Bonnie pressed herself against him. "Forget her, m'lord. I will warm your bed tonight."

He shoved her away. "I have told you, our time is done. Go and find another to ease your needs."

He stormed after Elena as Bonnie burst into loud tears and ran to the kitchen.

"Elena, stop!" he growled. She walked faster and with a muttered curse he chased after her.

"Dammit, girl, I said stop." He reached out and grabbed her arm, pulling her to a stop and twisting her around to face him.

"Leave me alone, Traven!" She tried to yank her arm free and when he wouldn't let her go, tried to punch him.

He grabbed both of her wrists and held them firmly. "Elena, I can explain."

"There is no need to explain!" She kicked him hard in the shin.

He grunted with pain as she glared at him. "It is perfectly clear, my lord. You have found someone more pleasant to share your bed tonight. Take your collar back. I am sure she will enjoy wearing it more than I."

She thrust her chin up, and with an angry snort he bent and picked her up, heaving her over his shoulder. He placed an iron arm across her legs, pinning her against him.

"Put me down, you brute!" she shouted.

She pounded on his back as he carried her down the hall. He carried her into the common room. It was emptier than it was at supper but there were still a few of his men sitting at the table, drinking and talking.

They looked up in surprise as Traven crossed the room. They watched with interest when he suddenly roared with pain. Elena had bitten him on the back, and he slapped her hard on her upturned ass as the other men raised their glasses and shouted laughter. He ignored them and carried Elena out of the room and up the stairs to his bedroom as she squirmed and flailed and shouted obscenities at him.

He carried her into the bedroom, slamming the door shut behind him before crossing to the bed. He sat down on it and slid her down onto his lap, her skirt hiking up around the tops of her thighs as she straddled him. She tried to hit him again and he pulled her arms behind her back, holding them firmly.

"Let me go!" She squirmed and wiggled and twisted on his lap for a few moments until she abruptly gave up, panting harshly and glaring at him.

"Are you finished?" He arched his eyebrow at her.

"I hate you!"

"Aye, you have mentioned that before." He ignored the sting he felt at her words.

Some of her hair had escaped her braid and, still holding her hands behind her back with his left hand, he brushed it back from her face with his right. She jerked her head away from his hand.

"Do not touch me, Traven!"

"She kissed me, Elena. I did not know she was going to kiss me, and I have no intention of taking her anywhere near my bed. I was on my way to find you when she cornered me."

"Cornered you? She is half your size, my lord, did she overpower you?" she sneered.

"I was pushing her away," he said patiently.

"It did not appear that way." Her voice was sulky. "You seemed to enjoy having her tongue in your mouth."

He gave her a sudden, delighted grin. "You are jealous."

"I am not," she responded indignantly.

"You are." He grinned again. "I know when a woman is jealous of another and you are."

She hissed at him like an angry cat, her nostrils flaring with annoyance and he laughed out loud. "Perhaps you do not hate me quite as much as you believe. In fact, I think -"

She slammed her mouth down on his, shoving her tongue angrily into his mouth then nipping his bottom lip hard.

He groaned and released her hands before cupping her ass and grinding her against his crotch as she threaded her fingers through his hair and yanked his head back. His grunt of pain turned into a low moan of excitement when she bent her head and licked his throat. She paused and then bit his neck hard enough to leave teeth marks. He roared with pain and grabbed her braid, pulling her head back.

He glared at her. "Brat! Are you trying to make me bleed?"

She grinned at him, a combination of lust and anger

glowing in her eyes. "You should not have kissed another then."

"I told you, she kissed me," he grumbled, cautiously releasing her as she moved her hands to the bottom of his shirt. He raised his arms so she could tug it off and drop it to the floor behind her. She trailed her fingers through the hair on his chest, and he groaned at the feel of her soft fingers. He cupped her breast and she immediately slapped his hand away.

He growled low in his throat and glared at her. She wound her fingers through his hair and pulled hard in response. "I agree to wear your collar and share your bed for a week, and yet I find you in the arms of another."

She leaned closer and traced his ear with her tongue. "It seems only fair that if you invite another into your bed then I am allowed to find my own pleasure with another."

He made a low sound of anger. "You are not to go near any man's bed but mine. Do you understand me, girl?"

She sucked hard on his earlobe in reply. This time when he slipped his hand under her shirt and cupped her bare breast, she didn't protest.

"Do you believe you are the only one being pursued by others? There are many men in your home who have invited me into their bed," she whispered into his ear.

"You deliberately try to provoke me, girl," he muttered. "I know you have been with no other since your husband. They call you the Ice Maiden, do they not?"

"Aye, they do." She planted soft kisses along the line of his jaw then kissed him hard on the mouth. He parted his lips so that she could slide her warm tongue into his mouth. She traced his teeth with her tongue, exploring his mouth leisurely as he squeezed and kneaded her breasts.

She pulled her mouth from his with a soft gasp and stared

down at him. "But it would appear your big cock has warmed the Ice Maiden."

He grinned arrogantly at her as she reached down and slipped her hand into his pants. She wrapped her fingers around his thick shaft and stroked it with long, firm pulls.

He moaned with pleasure before opening her shirt. He cupped her large breasts and sucked greedily on first one nipple and then the other. She arched her back, gasping when he scraped his teeth across her sensitive nipples.

"It does appear that you cannot resist my touch," he said with a smug grin before kissing her collarbone.

She shrugged and stopped stroking his large cock. "As I said before, your touch is pleasant enough, my lord. Now that you have reminded me how pleasant it is to have a man between my legs, perhaps after our week is done, I will show more interest in the other men who pursue me."

He froze against her. His hands left her breasts and moved around to cup her head. He held her firmly, thick tension growing between them.

His voice low and deliberate, he said, "If I see you wearing another's collar after our week is done," he traced his collar around her neck with one thick finger, "I will banish the man who it belongs to from my home. I will burn all of his possessions and leave him penniless and begging on the street. Do you understand me?"

ELENA STARED WIDE-EYED AT TRAVEN BEFORE SLOWLY pulling her hand out of his pants. Her heart was thumping and thudding, and the slow burn of anger was rising in her chest. "Traven, you cannot do that."

"I can and I will," he replied.

"You will tire quickly of me and move on to your next conquest," she said. "Am I supposed to spend the rest of my life alone? Have you done this to other women? Is this a condition for sharing your bed? That we can be with no other once you are finished with us?"

He shook his head. "No, only you, sweet Elena."

"Do not sweet Elena me! You have no right to play with my life this way. I work for you, I do not belong to you. You are mad if you think that I will stay away from other men once you have tired of me."

She tried to scramble free of his lap. He tugged her easily against his chest, cupping the back of her neck and guiding her ear to his mouth as she slapped at his back.

"I will never grow tired of you, Elena," he murmured into her ear.

She stiffened against him. "You will, my lord. You always do."

He shook his head and rubbed her bare back with his rough fingers. "I let a thief go just for the chance to have you in my bed again."

"Bryce did not steal your watch!" she said hotly.

He laughed. "It does not matter to me if he did or not. All that matters is that you are in my bed and wearing my collar the way you should be."

She bristled against him. "Only for a week."

He pulled on the collar, tugging her mouth down to his. He kissed her roughly and despite her anger with him, she couldn't help but return his kiss. God, what he did to her.

He released her mouth and rested his forehead against hers. "Do not take away the pleasure of your sweet body after only a week, Elena. I wish to have you for longer. Will you agree?"

She knew she surprised him when she said, "Aye, Traven, I will."

He gave her a delighted look, but she shook her head. "But only if you agree that I do not have to wear your collar around my neck."

He scowled. "That will never happen. My woman wears my collar. There will be no bargaining over that."

"Then our original agreement stands," she said. "One week – no more."

He leaned away from her and she could see the flash of hurt in his eyes. Why would he be hurt? He barely knew her and there were plenty of women in his household who would eagerly replace her.

She leaned forward to kiss him lightly on the lips. "I have hurt your feelings again, my lord. I am sorry."

He didn't reply and she sighed. Her anger had disappeared, leaving her tired and depressed, and she slipped off his lap. He made no move to stop her and she buttoned her shirt as she walked toward the door of his bedroom.

She was reaching for the handle when his hard hand fell on her arm. "Where are you going?"

She stared at him uncertainly. "Back to my room, my lord."

"You promised me a week."

She hesitated. "I thought you had lost your desire for me."

He laughed a little bitterly. "No, Elena, that has not happened."

He picked her up and carried her to his bed. He set her down gently beside it and stripped off first her clothes and then his own before he unbraided her hair. When it was loose around her shoulders, he reached out and traced the collar around her neck.

"You are mine for the next seven days, Elena," he said.

"There will be no house chores, no serving other men their dinner and their drink. You will not leave this bedroom unless I allow it. Your only job is to pleasure me. Do you understand?"

She nodded, and his eyes darkened with desire. "Good."

She stepped toward him and kissed the top of his shoulder. She traced her tongue across his throat and then nipped along his collarbone as he groaned and gripped her hips with hard fingers.

She trailed her fingers along the hard ridges of muscle in his stomach, liking the way he moaned when she dipped her fingers below his navel and ran them across his pubic bone. She continued to kiss his chest, bending a little so she could lick and suck on one flat nipple.

He groaned again and rubbed his cock along her thigh as she placed soft, wet kisses against his ribs. She pushed him backwards until he was sitting on the bed and then kneeled between his legs. Raw need pulsating through her, she studied his cock before bending her head. He moaned when her soft hair whispered across his thighs and jerked when she wrapped her warm lips around the head of his cock.

———

THE MOMENT ELENA'S MOUTH SLID OVER HIS COCK, TRAVEN was lost in an overwhelming sensation of pleasure. He moaned her name and twisted his hands into her hair as she bobbed her head up and down. When she swirled her tongue around the tip, he cried out and arched his hips against her.

He opened his eyes and looked down, his breath catching in his throat. Elena was staring up at him as she sucked his cock. Still staring at him, she slid her mouth agonizingly slow down his throbbing shaft. He watched his cock disappear into her mouth, felt her tongue lick the sensitive underside, and was helpless to stop his loud groan of pleasure.

"Oh my God, Elena," he moaned as she sucked and licked.

She released his cock and gave him a teasing grin. "Should I stop, Traven?"

"No, please," he begged. He pushed lightly on her head, silently urging her to continue and she smiled before sliding her mouth back down over his cock. He cried out with pleasure, moaning and panting as she pleasured him with her mouth.

After a few minutes she stood and climbed into his lap. She rested her knees on either side of his hips and raised her body, grasping his cock with one hand and guiding it into her pussy. She was dripping wet and they both groaned as his hard cock slid easily into her. He waited as she stretched around his thickness, kissing her throat and down the curve of her neck.

When she had stretched fully around him, she braced her hands on his broad shoulders and rocked back and forth. He leaned back on the bed, propping himself up on his elbows and watching hungrily as she spread her legs further and reached behind her to rest her hands on his thighs.

He stayed perfectly still as she braced her hands and lifted her pelvis up and down. She made a soft moan, and he clenched his teeth as she bounced faster and harder. He looked down, groaning as he watched his thick cock move in and out of her pussy. After only a few seconds, he looked away. Watching her take his cock into her body so easily made it nearly impossible for him not to come.

Elena was panting now, her face flushed and small breathless moans spilling from her lips as she thrust against him. She let her head fall back, her long dark hair tickling the tops of his thighs. He had to fight the urge to grab her around the hips and thrust wildly into her.

She stared up at the ceiling, her fingers digging into his thighs and rode him to a body-shuddering orgasm. He pulled her against his chest, and she collapsed against him, breathing harshly against his throat. He gave her a few moments to recover, brushing his fingers across her lower back and grimly ignoring the way her pussy clung wetly to his throbbing cock.

When her breathing had returned to normal, he gathered her hair into a ponytail and tugged her head back. He kissed her hard on the mouth, forcing his tongue between her lips. He kissed her hungrily, exploring every part of her mouth as he squeezed and kneaded her breasts. When she was moaning and rocking her hips against him again, he cupped her around the waist and lifted her from his lap.

She moaned in protest and reached down for his cock, but he was already standing and pushing her onto her hands and knees on his bed. He reached between her legs, rubbing his fingers across her clit and smiling when she spread her legs wide.

He kneeled on the bed behind her, positioned his cock at the entrance to her pussy and pushed into her. She cried out, her back arching as he bottomed out in her. He groaned at the feel of her wet tightness surrounding him and moved closer, pushing his thighs between hers until they were spread wide and her soft ass was resting against his pelvis. He placed one large hand on the small of her back and gathered her hair up with the other. He pushed down on her back and tugged her head back. She gasped and arched her back but made no protest, and he made a few slow, deep thrusts.

He wanted to go slowly, wanted to make the pleasure last as long as he could, but the sight of Elena on her hands and knees with his collar around her neck and her face flushed with pleasure, had his balls tightening almost immediately.

He put both hands around her hips and lifted. She shifted, burying her face into his bed and raising her ass up to give him better access. He thrust into her, pounding his body against hers and groaning loudly with every hard stroke. He could feel his orgasm coming and he reached under her to skate his fingers across her clit.

She cried out, the sound muffled in the sheets, and pushed her ass back against him. He was very close now and he rubbed her clit roughly as he plunged in and out of her. He gave a loud moan as he came, Elena shuddering beneath him as she came as well, and he pumped in and out a few more times before collapsing on his side on the bed beside her.

He wrapped his arm around her waist, pulling her shaking body up against his and brushing the hair back from her face. Her eyes were closed, and he studied her face for a few moments. She had a few freckles on her nose that he had never noticed before. He smiled and kissed the tip of her nose before studying the thickness of her eyelashes and the curve of her mouth.

She opened her eyes and blinked sleepily at him. "What, my lord?"

"Traven," he reminded her, shifting her closer.

"What, Traven?" She yawned and slipped her arm around his waist. She hesitated and then pulled her arm away. He frowned and pulled it back around him.

"You look sleepy, sweet Elena." He brushed his lips across hers.

"Aye, I am." She tried to shift away from him, and he pushed his leg between hers, putting his arm around her and resting one heavy hand against her lower back, refusing to let her move away.

"Go to sleep," he demanded.

He pulled her even closer, pushing her head against his broad chest. She burrowed her face into his shoulder, even as she muttered, "No sleeping, only fucking. Remember?"

He grunted and stroked her back with the tips of his fingers. "Go to sleep, girl. You will leave my bed only when I say you can."

He expected her to protest, perhaps to pop up and try to punch him again, but she only snuggled in closer and murmured, "Aye, my lord."

CHAPTER 7

Traven watched as Elena lifted her face to the sun. It was cold out, but the sun was shining brightly, and he could see the pleasure in her face even from across the yard.

"Four days, Traven. That is a record – even for you."

He grinned a little at the sound of Duncan's voice behind him.

"Has it been that long?" He continued to watch Elena as she picked her way carefully across the frozen ground toward the stables.

"Aye. We were beginning to think you would spend the entire seven days in your bed with her." Duncan didn't even try to hide the amusement in his voice.

He shrugged. "It has been a long time since I have been with a woman."

"Indeed. It is a wonder the poor girl can even walk," Graham said.

Traven turned around to face Graham and Duncan. Duncan was grinning at him in an amused sort of way, but Graham had arranged his face into a polite mask.

"Hot baths and healing oil can do wonders for a woman," Traven said.

Duncan rolled his eyes before clapping him on the back. "I should not be surprised that you would be the one to warm the Ice Maiden. You always did have a way with the ladies." He paused. "You are handsome enough, but I dare say it is the rumour of your big cock that entices them so."

Traven could feel a blush rising in his face and Duncan roared with laughter. Elena glanced briefly at them before disappearing into the stables.

"My lord," Graham said with a brittle smile, "perhaps now would be a good time to discuss what has been happening in your absence. Although, I am willing to continue in my current position if you are too busy with your Ice Maiden or require longer to recover from your time spent in battle."

"That is kind of you, Graham," Traven said. "But I am more than capable of handling my own affairs. Come, old friend, we will have breakfast while we talk."

He led the older man toward the castle as Duncan walked on to the stables.

ELENA RUBBED THE LARGE NECK OF THE HORSE BEFORE reaching for some carrot that was in a bag hanging from the stall door. She put it in the palm of her hand and offered it to the horse. He chuffed happily and then crunched it between his large teeth. She ran her fingers through his mane, gently pulling out the tangles as the horse snuffled at her neck with its large nose.

She smiled a little. The horse belonged to Traven. The beast was the very one that he had brought her back to the castle on. She shivered a little at the memory of riding the horse while Traven had touched and caressed her.

She closed her eyes and buried her face in the horse's warm neck. There were only three days left in her agreement with Traven and already the thought of leaving his warm bed was forming a knot of dread in her belly. The last four days had passed in a blur of sex and sleeping and eating. She had done nothing at all but pleasure Traven and sleep in his bed. He had their meals brought to his bedroom and it was the first time in four days that she had even set foot outside of his room.

She had never had so much sex in her life, she thought ruefully. Neither of them could get enough of each other, and she wondered if this was the way it always was with Traven in the beginning. She sighed, thinking about the way he'd so sweetly carried in buckets of hot water for the tub for her, instead of asking a servant to do it, and the time he'd spent rubbing and massaging his healing oil into her flesh.

Considering how long it had been since she used those particular muscles and considering the seemingly endless variety of positions that Traven fucked her in, she was surprised and a little impressed with how quickly her body had adapted to the surge of unexpected exercise.

Not that she wasn't sore. This morning Traven had pinned her against the wall, spreading her legs wide and fucking her hard and fast until she was crying out with pleasure and raking her nails down his broad back.

She reached behind her and rubbed her lower back. At the time, neither of them had noticed or paid any attention to the jagged piece of rock on the stone wall. It wasn't until they had finished and collapsed on his bed that she noticed the throbbing.

Traven had examined her back, cursing under his breath

at the small but deep scrape on her pale skin. He'd washed it carefully, murmuring an apology at her hiss of pain. He applied some type of salve to the small wound, it had a strong and unpleasant odor, but he ignored her protests and pushed aside her hands, putting the salve on with gentle fingers.

"It smells," she complained, her nose wrinkling

He laughed and kissed her on the forehead. "It will help prevent infection and help your skin to heal."

"How do you know all of this?"

He shrugged. "There are thousands of injuries in a war. You learn quickly how to try and heal them."

She ran gentle fingers down the scar on his face. His body was covered with small scars, with a larger one running from his left knee down to his ankle, and she noticed that when he was very tired, he limped slightly.

She had asked him about it, and he'd grunted and shook his head. "I do not wish to speak of the war, sweet Elena. It is done and I would forget my memories of it as quickly as possible."

She nodded and not asked him about it again. On the second night, when he woke her by moaning and talking in his sleep, she gathered him closer to her and rubbed his back soothingly until the nightmare passed and he was sleeping deeply again.

He was quiet and withdrawn in the morning, but she did not bring up the nightmare. Instead she knelt between his legs, licking and sucking his cock until, moaning loudly, he came in her mouth.

That cheered him up considerably, she thought with amusement as the horse snuffed at her neck again. She handed it another piece of carrot, the smile abruptly dropping from her face. She'd spent four days in Traven's bed, and in many ways been more intimate with him than her husband, yet she still knew nothing about him. They'd spent the time exploring and discovering each other's body, not conversing. Still, his sweetness to her in the last four days had almost lulled her into believing they had some type of relationship.

You do not, she told herself fiercely. *It is just sex. He will grow tired of you, most likely any day now, and you need to remember that. Keep your head out of the clouds, girl.*

"Elena?"

She turned to see Bryce standing behind her. "Bryce? What are you doing here?"

She looked him up and down. It might have been her imagination, but his thin face seemed a bit fuller to her and instead of his usual shirt and torn pants, he was dressed warmly with a heavy jacket and a scarf and gloves.

He grinned at her and pulled the cap on his head down more firmly. "Lord Traven hired me as a stable boy."

"What?" She gaped at him.

He grinned again at her surprise. "Aye, that is what he wanted to speak to me about. He took me to the stables and when he saw how good I was with the horses, he offered me a job."

He gave her another proud smile. "He said if I worked hard and did not steal anything, he would teach me to ride and would talk to Neilan about letting me become his apprentice."

"That is good news, Bryce," Elena said.

"Aye," he agreed. He put his arm around her waist and rested his head against her arm. "He gave me new clothes and I have my own room and three meals a day and I get paid." He paused. "I am going to buy a sword and ask lord Traven to teach me to fight."

Elena frowned. "Bryce, you are only eleven. There is plenty of time to learn to fight."

He shrugged. "Aye, I guess so."

"When I was his age, I had already learned how to use a sword." A gravelly voice said behind them.

They turned to see Duncan standing there, one hand clasped loosely around the handle of his sword.

"If learning to fight is what you want, boy, we will teach you." Duncan raised one eyebrow at Bryce. "But first you will learn discipline and respect for the iron." He pulled the sword from his belt and handed it to Bryce. "Clean and sharpen this – Rayden the blacksmith will show you how – and bring it back to me."

Bryce took the sword and nodded solemnly to Duncan. As he walked past Elena, she put her hand on his shoulder, pulling him to a stop and kissing him on the forehead. He frowned and glanced at Duncan before giving her a look that clearly indicated she was embarrassing him.

She laughed and kissed him again. "Go on, Bryce. I will see you later."

He walked quickly out of the stables, nodding when Duncan called after him, "And do not run with that sword, boy."

He turned back to Elena, eyeing her up and down. "Hello, Elena."

"Hello, Duncan."

"How are you?"

"Very well," she replied. "It is a beautiful day out, is it not?"

"Aye. I imagine you are glad to see the sun and get a bit of fresh air."

She blushed, and he grinned at her. "Have you seen Aldina yet?"

"No. I am going to the kitchen now to find her."

"She will be happy to see you. She has been pining for

you these last four days." He grinned again as her blush deepened.

He held his arm out to her. "Come, girl, I will tease you no longer. Let me escort you to the kitchen."

She linked her arm around his as he led her from the stables. He glanced at the collar around her neck and she stared thoughtfully at him. "Duncan, may I ask you a question?"

"You may."

"Earlier, you seemed surprised to see the lord Enderson's collar around my throat. Yet you were there when we made the bargain, I saw you."

When he didn't reply, she prompted him. "Why were you surprised, Duncan?"

"My surprise was not that you were wearing his collar but in the collar itself."

"What do you mean?"

"The collar you are wearing belonged to his mother."

"It is not unusual for a mother to pass her collar down to her son."

"No," he admitted, "it is not. But Traven has never allowed another to wear it."

She stopped and gave him a look of disbelief. "What?"

"Until you, the only woman who wore that collar was his mother. It was the first collar her husband gifted to her and her favourite. When it was passed to Traven, he tucked it away and had the other one made. He has never given his mother's collar to a woman to wear."

She swallowed, her hand tracing the worn leather around her throat. "He said I had a choice."

She gave Duncan a horrified look, "I should not have picked this one, but I did not know its importance. He only said I could choose between them. If I had known how special it was to him, I would have chosen the other."

Duncan shrugged. "Obviously he hoped you would wear it, or he would not have given you a choice."

She shook her head. "He knew how much I despised the other. It is the only reason he gave me the choice."

"I would not be so sure of that, Elena. It is not in Traven's nature to bend to a woman's will."

"Aye, I suppose it is not," Elena said.

They were nearing the castle and as the sun touched on Duncan's face, she studied him closely. "Duncan, are you unwell?"

"I feel fine. Why?"

"You look," she hesitated, "a little tired." Her gaze slipped to his ribs. "Does your injury bother you?"

"No. It is fully healed and has been for some time." He lifted his shirt and showed her the wide scar that ran from just below his armpit to his hip.

Duncan was long and lean, the muscles in his abdomen standing out in sharp relief against his skin. He was very handsome, she mused, with his long dark hair and green eyes. Compared to Traven's intensity, he had an easy-going nature and was quick to smile and tease. She knew many of the women in Traven's estate desired him, but if the servant rumours were true, Duncan had not taken up any of them on their offer to slate his desire. As far as she knew, he hadn't taken a woman to his bed since he returned from the war.

Of course, he'd been nearly dead when the wagon had pulled up in front of the castle. Infection had set in, and if it hadn't been for Aldina's care and the many herb potions she had forced down his throat, he would have died.

"It looks much better," she said.

He grimaced. "Aye, I suppose it does. I am lucky to be

alive. If it were not for Traven's decision to send me home and Aldina's wretched tasting potions, I would be worm food by now."

She squeezed his arm. "Duncan, will you tell me what's wrong? I know we do not know each other that well, but I can see something troubles you."

"Just," he paused, "restless, I suppose. It happens to all men from time to time."

They had reached the castle and he gave her a smile that looked forced. "Go and visit with Aldina. She will be glad to see you."

ELENA CURLED UP AGAINST TRAVEN'S SIDE AS HE LAID ON HIS back. He kept his arm around her, stroking her back lightly as she pulled the covers up around them. She burrowed herself into his warmth and sighed contently.

Traven had given her the entire day to spend with Aldina and the other servants. She visited and helped with the chores around the house, catching up on the gossip as she cleaned. A few of the other servants grinned and teased her repeatedly throughout the day, but she accepted their good-natured teasing and refused to answer any of their questions about both the size of Traven's cock or his abilities in bed.

At one point she expressed her surprise to Aldina over their endless questioning. "Surely, most of them have already slept with lord Traven," she said. "His lust for women is common knowledge, is it not?"

Aldina shrugged. "Aye, but most of the women he has slept with are no longer working in his household."

She gave Aldina a look of horror. "Are you telling me that

once he has grown tired of them, he no longer allows them to work for him?"

"No, Traven would never do that. But the women do not wish to continue working for him if they can no longer share his bed. I believe Bonnie is the only servant left who has slept with Traven. The rest have moved on to different households."

She gave Elena a sudden, hard look. "He is a heart-breaker, Elena. Do not forget that. As kind as he is to you now, as obsessed as he is with you, he will grow tired of you. I have seen it many times over the years. He is a good man, but he will not fall in love with you."

"Aye, Aldina, I will not forget," Elena replied.

Aldina's expression softened. "I do not say this to hurt you. I wish only to protect you." She paused. "Lord Enderson is different since returning from the war, but I do not believe that he will ever be satisfied with one woman. Men like him rarely are. Do not give him your heart."

"I appreciate your concern, but I am not a naive, young girl. I know that he is using me and will grow tired of me soon," she said. "Besides, you forget that I do this only because of Bryce. Three more days and I will leave his bed of my own accord."

She ran her fingers over the collar around her throat and stared blankly out the window. "The sooner I can remove his collar, the better."

Aldina didn't reply and Elena glanced at her. "What do you mean when you say he is different?"

Aldina shook the sheet out and Elena helped her tuck it in around the bed. "He is more solemn and quieter now. When he left for the war, he was loud and bold and impulsive, and quick to laugh – still very much a boy really. Now," she hesitated, "even my David has noticed a change in him, and you know that David never notices anything."

She sighed and handed the top sheet to Elena. "The night that Farlan spoke improperly to you – the old lord Traven would never have reacted in that manner. He would not have nearly killed one of his own men for speaking to his woman that way."

Elena frowned. "He would not have killed Farlan."

Aldina cocked her head at her, "Are you so sure, Elena? If you had not intervened, had not coaxed him into the kitchen with you, I believe Farlan would have died by his hand that day."

"You are wrong," Elena said. "Traven would not kill a man over something as small as that."

Aldina stared thoughtfully at her. "I thought it was the war that changed him, but perhaps it is you. Perhaps he is ready to settle down with a woman."

Elena snorted loudly. "He is not, trust me. He has no interest in me other than how I can pleasure him physically."

Just after dinner, as Elena was helping the other servants to clear the table, Traven stood and without speaking, held his hand out to her. She went to him without protest, allowing him to lead her to his bedroom where he immediately stripped her naked and unbraided her hair. He pulled a blanket from the bed and draped it on the floor in front of the fireplace. He laid her down in front of the fire and spent the next few hours teasing and touching her soft skin, coaxing orgasm after orgasm from her willing body until he finally slipped between her legs and sated his own lust for her.

He carried her to the bed and now, curled up against him, Elena wrapped her arm more tightly across his narrow waist and waited for the familiar sound of his soft snoring to begin.

To her surprise, instead of drifting off like he normally did, he said, "Do your parents still live?"

She stared up at him and he smoothed a stray piece of hair away from her face. "No, my lord. They died many years ago."

He gave her an irritable look. "Traven. How many times must I remind you to call me Traven when you are in my bed, Elena?"

She rolled her eyes in response and he slapped her lightly on the ass, making her giggle. He smiled at her laughter before sobering. "How did they die?"

She shrugged. "I do not know. My uncle woke me early one morning and told me that my parents were dead. He brought me to his home, and I lived with him and my aunt until I married my husband."

"You were not given the chance to say goodbye, or to see their bodies? You were not given any explanation at all for their deaths?" His voice was shocked.

She shrugged again. "I was very young, Traven. I believe my uncle did not wish to traumatize me."

"He did not tell you even when you grew older?" Traven asked.

"I asked a few times and he told me dwelling on the past was a foolish habit."

He grunted angrily. "Do you have siblings?"

"No. My aunt and uncle had seven children though. Most of them were many years older than me, but I was occasionally allowed to play with their youngest Sephina. She was my age."

"What do you mean, allowed to play?"

She raised herself up a little and stared at him. "I was a servant in their home, Traven."

"What?" he nearly shouted. "How old were you when your parents died?"

"I was six."

His mouth dropped open and he sat up, scowling down at her as she wrapped the sheet around her nakedness and sat cross-legged beside him.

"They made a six-year-old a servant? Their own flesh and blood was forced to work in their home?"

She bristled a little. "I was big for my age and had been helping my mother clean our house. I was more than capable of doing it."

"Elena," he cupped her arms, "that is not the point. The point is they made a child work as a slave."

She laughed. "Traven, you are too dramatic. They treated me well enough, gave me clothing and food and allowed me to live in their home for many years. My mother was not close to her brother, he could have left me to beg in the streets."

"It is not right," he repeated.

She gave him a solemn look. "I owe them my life, Traven. If they had not taken me in, I would have died on the streets in less than a week." She brightened. "For a while they even let me sit in with Sephina during her studies. They are quite wealthy, and they had a nanny and a tutor for their children. I learned the letters and numbers and a few words just from listening in on her studies. It only lasted a few weeks though. Sephina found my presence distracting and my uncle decided it was a waste of my time."

"You cannot read?" He stared flabbergasted at her and she blushed brightly.

"I know the letters and numbers," she muttered in embarrassment before looking down at the sheets.

He tipped her chin up. "Do you know who Danai is?"

She nodded. Although Traven's estate was large, she had been there long enough to know just about everyone who lived within its walls. Danai was an old woman who spent most of her days sitting quietly by the fire in the common room, usually with a book in her hand. She was pleasant and soft-spoken, and children were drawn to her like bees to honey.

Elena had never gotten it straight if she was a relative of Traven's or just someone special to him, but she knew the other servants in his home treated her with a gentle type of respect. Even lord Barten was polite to her.

"Danai was my nanny and tutor when I was a child." He rubbed his thumb across her bottom lip. "I will speak with her tomorrow about teaching you to read and write."

She gasped and raised her knees to her chest, hugging them like a small child would. "Truly, Traven?"

He grinned at the obvious delight in her voice. "Aye."

She leaned forward, cupping his face and kissing him soundly on the mouth. "Thank you, Traven. I have always wanted to learn to read and write."

"You are welcome, sweet Elena." He laid back down on the bed and she curled up next to him again.

He stared at the ceiling, as she rubbed her hand across his chest. "Do you have any siblings?"

"Aye, I have a sister. She lives nearly three days ride from here."

"Are you close to her?"

"Not really. She is older than me and married her husband at a young age. It has been many years since we lived close to each other."

She tried not to sigh when he brought the subject back to her childhood. "Did you have toys as a child? Did they give you any opportunity to play?"

She could hear the anger in his voice, and she rubbed his chest soothingly. "I told you, my lord, I was occasionally allowed to play with Sephina."

"Were you given toys?"

"I had a few dolls that I fashioned from sticks and some fabric. Sephina let me play with her dollhouse once. It was so beautiful. It was very large and had many rooms, and my uncle hired a man to build all the furniture. There were chairs and beds and tables, and even dishes and cutlery, no bigger than my thumbnail. My aunt hired a woman to sew draperies for the windows and quilts for the beds and tiny dishtowels."

She gave him a slightly guilty look. "It was my job to dust it and sometimes, if there were no others around, I would play with it for a bit. My aunt caught me playing with it one day."

She stared down at the bed quilt. "I was given a beating for my disobedience. I stopped playing with it after that, but I still remember how much I wished it was mine. It was so lovely."

He grunted angrily and she rubbed his chest again. "It was a long time ago." She suddenly smiled at him. "I had a kitten once."

He returned her smile. "Did you?"

"Aye. He was a stray that wandered into my uncle's yard. He was so cute. He was orange with stripes, and he had fuzzy long hair."

"What happened to him?"

"I kept him hidden for a while, but once Sephina discovered him, she desired him for herself. My uncle made me give him to her." Her face darkened. "When Sephina tired of him after a few weeks, my uncle gave him away to a peddler who was passing through. Anyway, it is late, we should get some sleep."

Traven stared at the ceiling as Elena curled against him, her warm breath stirring his chest hair. He had never realized until this moment how lucky he'd been to grow up in a home of wealth. Listening to Elena speak so matter-of-factly about her horrible childhood was making him ashamed of his callous disregard for the privileges that had been afforded to him.

"Traven?" Elena's soft voice interrupted his thoughts. "Are you angry with me?"

He shook his head and kissed her roughly on the forehead, "No, girl, I am not angry with you. I am angry with your uncle for treating you so poorly and upset that you had such a terrible childhood."

She sighed and sat up again. "Traven, he did not treat me poorly, and my childhood was perfectly fine. I could have been like poor Bryce whose parents abandoned him when he was just a young boy. Do you know he has been living on his own on the street since he was eight?" She paused. "Thank you for hiring him to work in your household."

He nodded but persisted with his belief about her childhood. "Elena, your childhood was not perfectly fine. Children should play and run and be given the opportunity to learn to read and write."

She smiled a little. "My lord, not everyone is as lucky as you."

"How did you meet your husband?" His body tensed as he waited for her answer. He didn't want to know about the man she had loved, but he *had* to know.

"He was hired by my uncle to be his blacksmith. We fell in love quickly and were married less than a year later," Elena said.

"What happened then?"

"William never liked that my uncle did not pay me for my service to his household. Once we were married, he demanded that I be paid a fair wage. When my uncle refused, William quit, and we left. We were hired by the lord Barten and joined your household."

"How far away is your uncle's home from here?"

"Not far," she replied. "A half day's ride, maybe a little more. They travel through here from time to time and will stop and visit."

"How long were you married before your husband died?" he asked.

"Nearly two years." She stared down at her hands which were clasped together in her lap. "He became ill and died after only a few days."

"I am sorry for your loss," he said gruffly.

She smiled at him. "Thank you, Traven. He was a good man, my William."

"Why have you not been with any other?"

She shrugged. "No one else appealed to me. And while my husband understood my desire to not wear a collar, I have yet to meet anyone else who does."

A strange buzzing filled his head. "Have you never worn a collar until now?"

"No." The shame was back in her eyes and she cleared her throat nervously, picking at an invisible thread on the blanket.

He stared at her in shock. His collar was the only one that had graced her neck and that knowledge filled him with a fierce type of possessiveness, but he was suddenly deeply ashamed at the way he had baited her into wearing it. If it had not been for the beggar boy, she would never have agreed to wear it. He had been so used to women nearly begging to wear his collar, so determined to see his collar around Elena's neck and claim her as his own, that he had not given any thought to how it might make her feel.

He had hoped that even after their agreement was done, she would agree to continue to wear his collar but looking at her now, seeing the shame in her eyes, he knew the chance of her agreeing to it were slim. The thought filled him with depression, and he sighed and turned away from her.

"You are right, it is late," he said as he blew the candles out next to the bed and pulled the covers up to his shoulders. "Go to sleep, girl."

"Good night, my lord." Her voice was quiet, but he could hear the worry and disappointment in it. He glanced over his shoulder at her, but the darkness of the room and the way she had curled up on her side away from him, meant he couldn't see her face.

It was the first night that he hadn't wrapped her in his embrace to sleep and he wondered if she felt as alone and miserable as he did. Of course, in two more days they would be sleeping in separate beds again. Perhaps, it was wise to get used to being alone again.

He lay silently with his back turned to her, listening to her soft breathing, a war storming inside of him. After only a few moments, he turned over and pulled her into his arms. She curled into him, wrapping her arm around his waist as he tucked her soft curves against him.

"Good night, Traven." She kissed his chest hesitantly and he cupped her face and kissed her soft lips.

"Good night, Elena."

CHAPTER 8

Traven slammed the door and strode through the cold air toward the stables. He'd been in a foul mood since he woke on the eighth day to find himself alone in his bed. He had checked the box sitting on the table next to the door, his hands clenching into fists when he'd seen the collar nestled carefully in it.

Now, over a week later, he was not just angry but tired and miserable as well. He hadn't slept well since Elena left his bed and despite his best intentions, he was taking it out on the people around him.

He refused to speak to Elena and ignored her completely. After her initial timid hello, she had avoided him. He knew he was being childish, knew he was acting like a spoiled little boy who wasn't getting his way, but he couldn't seem to help it.

The first night she served dinner without his collar around her neck, one of his men was foolish enough to grab her ass. Traven had slammed his mug of mead on the table, shattering the hard glass and splashing mead everywhere. The entire room quieted as Traven stared at the man, his nostrils flaring angrily. After a tense moment where Traven seriously considered cutting both the man's hand and dick off, the man removed his hand from Elena's ass. The room stayed quiet for a few seconds more before slowly filled up with soft conversation.

Aldina and Elena cleaned up the puddle of mead without speaking. He had to force himself not to throw Elena over his shoulder and carry her to his room when she knelt beside him to wipe up the mead on the floor and her sweet scent filled his nostrils.

Since that moment, not a single man in his household had gone near her, despite her lack of collar. It was the only thing that had brought him comfort since she left his bed.

"Traven?"

"What is it, Duncan?" He stopped and, although he had no wish for conversation, waited for him to catch up.

"One of your men is in trouble."

He sighed and rubbed at his forehead. "What kind of trouble?"

"He raped one of the women in the village just south of here."

He swung around and stared at Duncan. "Who was it?"

"Ragor." Duncan's face was an angry mask.

Traven thought carefully. "He is one of the men that Graham hired, correct? The big, fat one with the missing front teeth?"

"Aye."

"The woman's father has vowed to cut off his head. He almost caught the fat bastard too, but Ragor slithered away and has returned."

"Returned," Traven said blankly. "You jest, Duncan."

"I do not," Duncan said. "He sits in the common room, belching and drinking and acting like he has not a care in the world." A look of disgust passed over Duncan's face. "Graham has assured him that he will not be punished, and he is safe here behind the walls of your estate."

"I knew I would find you here, Duncan." Graham's voice was low and filled with anger as he joined them. "Running like an obedient dog to his master."

Duncan's hand dropped to the handle of his sword and Traven put a staying hand on his arm. "Graham, is what Duncan says true?"

Graham folded his arms behind his back and made a careless shrug. "Ragor told me the woman asked for it. That she _"

"I saw the woman," Duncan snapped. "Do you really think she asked to be beaten? To be violated in such a terrible way by the smelly swine you call a friend?"

"He is not my friend," Graham said. "I hired him to do a job. A job he does very well." His gaze switched to Traven. "He protects your estate, Traven. What he does in his free time should not matter."

"Should not matter?" Traven glared at Graham. "Have you gone mad, Graham? He raped a woman. We do not harbor men like him behind the walls of my home."

"He says he did not rape her. It is his word against hers. We are not judge and jury, Traven. We cannot punish him without knowing the true facts. If we cast him outside the walls, he will last a matter of days before this woman's father finds him. Are you ready to do that to a man who may be innocent?" Graham asked.

Traven glanced at Duncan. His friend shook his head. "He is not innocent. There were witnesses who watched him drag her into the trees."

"Other women," Graham said in disdain. "You would believe the word of women over one of your own men?"

Traven studied Graham until the older man flushed but gave Traven a defiant look. "Again, Traven, you would cast this man out, knowing full well that he will die within a matter of days?"

Traven gave him a tight grin. "You are right, Graham. I would not be so cruel as to allow him to suffer."

"Traven, he is guilty. He did -"

Traven held up his hand. "Enough, Duncan. I have made my decision."

Graham gave him a smug smile. "It is a wise one, Traven."

"Indeed." Traven turned to Duncan. "You and Henry will take Ragor and deliver him to the woman's father."

"Traven," Graham said as a smile crept across Duncan's face, "you said you would not cast him out."

"No, old friend," Traven said. "I said I would not allow him to suffer. Casting him out will mean a week of hiding, starving, running… until he is captured." A smile crossed his face. "Think of how I ease Ragor's suffering by delivering him directly to the woman's father. He will lose his head on a full stomach, rather than an empty one. Perhaps he will wish to thank me for my kindness. What do you think, Duncan?"

"Aye, Traven. I am sure he will," Duncan replied with a broad grin.

"You cannot do this, Traven," Graham's voice was rough with anger. "Ragor is -"

"Ragor is a filthy swine who is not fit to bear the crest of my family," Traven said. "I have made my decision on this matter, Graham, and you would be wise to hold your tongue. My patience runs thin today."

Graham's nostrils flared but he gave Traven a stiff smile before turning and stalking away. Traven waited until he was out of earshot before shaking his head. "What has happened to him, Duncan? I have known Graham since I was a boy. He is a few years older than me, but we were always friends. I believed I was doing the right thing leaving him in command while I went to war. But I do not remember him being so, so…"

"Foolish and cruel?"

"Aye." Traven rubbed at his forehead wearily.

"Are you all right, Traven?" Duncan asked.

He nodded. "Aye, just tired."

"And missing the Ice Maiden's presence in your bed, I suspect," Duncan said.

"I cannot get her out of my head," Traven said. He could hear the longing in his voice, and he was ashamed by it but unable to hide it. "She is all I think about, all I see when I close my eyes at night. I cannot sleep, I cannot eat… I fear I am going insane."

Duncan clapped him on the back. "My father once told me many years ago, that falling in love was akin to going insane."

Traven gave him a startled look. "I do not love Elena. I barely know her."

Duncan shrugged. "She is inside your head, my friend. If that is not love, then what is?"

"I do not… you speak foolishly, Duncan," Traven said. "Go and take the swine Ragor to his fate, would you? Just the thought of him sitting at my table fills me with anger."

"Aye, Traven. Are you sure you do not want to go with me and watch them remove his head from his disgusting body?"

Traven shook his head. "No, I need to go for a ride, need to clear my head."

"All right. Be safe."

"Aye, I will." He walked into the stable and hollered for Bryce.

The young boy popped his head up out of a stall. "Good morning, m'lord."

"Saddle my horse, boy. Be quick about it," he said.

"Yes, my lord." Bryce quickly saddled his horse and Traven led the beast out of the stable. He swung into the saddle and gave Bryce a brief nod of thanks before clucking to his horse. He rode toward the gate, his desire to get away growing inside of him. Jameson opened the gate and Traven nosed his horse through the opening and rode away.

HE RETURNED HOURS LATER. DARK HAD FALLEN LONG AGO, and he was cold and tired and hungry. He rode into the stable, frowning when Bryce did not appear, and quickly brushed and fed his horse before crossing the yard to his home. He slipped inside. The castle was quiet and dark, most people had gone to bed hours ago. He walked toward the kitchen. He would have a bite to eat and retire to his room.

As he approached the kitchen, he could see the flicker of candlelight, hear the low muttering of voices. He paused at the open doorway and listened.

"We have to tell him. If he does not see her, he will ask about her," Duncan said quietly.

"He will kill him." Aldina squeezed David's hand and stared worriedly at her husband.

The short, balding man shrugged. "He deserves to die for what he tried to do to her, Aldina."

"I do not disagree, but she will not want him to -"

Aldina gave a frightened squeak as Traven stepped into the light. "What is going on?"

There was silence and he stared at Duncan. "Tell me what has happened."

Duncan stood. "It is Elena."

"What about her?" Fear was unfurling in his belly as he stared at Duncan's white face.

"Earlier this evening, Elena was – she was -"

"What Duncan?" he nearly shouted.

"She was attacked, lord Traven," David said.

He stared at Aldina's husband, his heart pounding in his chest so hard it felt like he was being kicked repeatedly by his horse. "Does she live?"

"Yes, my lord," Aldina said immediately. "She is alive. Lord Barten sent for the doctor. He is with her now. She has a dislocated shoulder and bruised ribs, but he says she will live. He has given her something for the pain and in a few moments, he is going to try and put her shoulder back in place."

"Where is she?" Traven said hoarsely.

"In her room," Aldina said.

He turned and ran for the servant quarters, the others hurrying behind him. He pushed open the door of her room and ran to her bedside. A thin, gray-haired man was sitting on the bed beside her, holding her wrist in his hand. Graham stood at the end of her bed, his face hidden in the shadows, as Traven fell to his knees beside her bed.

"Elena," he whispered. He stared horrified at her. Her tanned face was pale and swollen. He could see the beginning of a black eye, and her lower lip was swollen to twice its size with a large cut on it.

"Hello, my lord," she whispered.

His hand shaking, he smoothed her hair back from her face. "I am so sorry, my sweet Elena."

She shook her head and winced before clearing her throat. "It is not your fault, Traven."

She closed her eyes and Traven glanced at the doctor. "Have you put her shoulder back into place?"

"Not yet, my lord. I was just about to." He glanced at Graham. "I will need assistance, lord Barten. Can you - "

"I will help you," Traven said. Graham scowled but stayed silent as the doctor twisted a large towel into a rope.

The doctor glanced up at the others. "Clear the room, please."

Aldina shook her head. "I will stay as well. You may need me."

As the others filed out of the room, Traven caught movement in the corner. He squinted past the candlelight, staring at the boy who sat there. "Bryce, go to the kitchen with the others."

The boy didn't move. "No, I am not leaving her."

Traven sighed impatiently. "Do not argue with me, boy. Go to the kitchen."

"No, I will not!" Bryce stood and stared at him defiantly, his small hands curled into fists.

"Bryce, come here, my love," Elena whispered.

Bryce ran to the bed and stared worriedly at her.

"Would you go to the kitchen and make me some tea? I am very thirsty." She tried to smile at him, and Traven winced when a trickle of blood oozed out of the cut on her lip.

"Aye, Elena. I can do that."

"Thank you, love." She closed her eyes again and Bryce hesitated before kissing her on the forehead. He scurried out of the room and Duncan gave Traven a reassuring nod before closing the door and leaving them alone.

The doctor leaned over Elena. "Elena?"

She opened her eyes and stared wearily at him.

"This is going to hurt, but we must put your shoulder back into place. Do you understand?"

"Aye."

The doctor squeezed her hand and stared at Traven and Aldina. "Are you ready? We must do this quickly."

The two of them nodded and the doctor said, "Help me sit her up."

AN HOUR LATER, THE OTHERS LOOKED UP AS TRAVEN, carrying Elena in his arms, passed by the kitchen with the doctor following closely behind him. Aldina stepped into the kitchen. Her usual ruddy face was pale, and her hands were shaking as she crossed the room and hugged David.

"How is she?" Duncan swallowed hard. "We – we heard her screaming."

Aldina leaned against David. "We got her shoulder back into place. The doctor believes she will be completely healed in a few weeks.

"That is good news." David kissed her forehead.

"Where is Traven taking her?" Graham asked.

"To his room," Aldina replied.

"Is that wise?" Graham frowned. "Perhaps it would be better if she stays in her own bed. What if he accidentally hurts her in the night?"

"He would not hurt her!" Bryce glared at the blonde man.

Before Graham could reply, Traven returned to the kitchen.

"Who did this to her?" His voice was low and filled with rage.

Duncan stood. "Traven, you should take a moment to -"

"Who did this to her, Duncan? You will tell me what I want to know now!"

"It was Farlan," Duncan said.

"Farlan," Traven repeated.

"Aye. He cornered her in the stables and – and attacked her."

"Did he rape her?"

"She says he did not," Aldina replied.

"I tried to help her, my lord. I swear to you I did," Bryce said.

Traven stared at the large bruise rising on the boy's cheek. "Tell me what happened, boy."

"I heard her screaming and I ran into the stall to find him on top of her. He was – was punching her and I jumped on his back." The young boy suddenly grinned ferociously. "I bit off his earlobe, my lord, and it made him stop punching her."

Traven stared at the boy. "What happened then?"

Bryce scowled. "I do not know. He threw me into the side of the stall and that is the last thing I remember."

"Neilan heard Elena's screams and Bryce's shouts. He pulled Farlan from her, but the bastard slipped free from him and ran," Duncan said.

"He is gone?" The scowl on Traven's face deepened.

"I have sent two men to search for him," Graham said.

"Send more." Traven's voice was cold. "You tell them to do whatever it takes to find him. I do not care if they have to go to the ends of the earth – they are to find him and bring him back to me alive. Do you understand, Graham?"

"Aye, Traven."

"Then go," Traven snarled.

Graham left the kitchen as Traven turned his gaze to Bryce. "Go to my room and have the doctor examine your head before he leaves."

As Bryce walked by him, Traven ruffled his hair. "You did well, boy. Thank you."

Bryce flushed with pleasure and gave Traven a shy grin before leaving.

———

"HOW ARE YOU FEELING, MY SWEET?" TRAVEN WHISPERED AS he slid carefully into the bed beside Elena.

"Sore." She groaned as she tried to move into a more comfortable position.

"Can you eat something?" he asked anxiously.

"No, I only want to sleep please. I am so tired, Traven." Her voice was slurred from a combination of the pain and the medication the doctor had given her.

He kissed her forehead. "I will be right here beside you if you need anything."

"Thank you. Could you help me turn to my side? I cannot sleep on my back."

"Of course." He helped her move on to her uninjured side, whispering apologies when she cried out from the pain.

She was panting and moaning softly by the time he had her positioned on her side. He hovered over her helplessly. "What can I do, sweet Elena?"

"Hold me," she whispered.

"I do not want to hurt you."

"You will not," she whimpered. "Please, Traven." Her voice was becoming softer and slower as she drifted towards sleep. "I have missed your touch so much."

He laid down beside her, resting his chest against her bare back, and carefully slid his arm around her waist. Her injured arm was bandaged against her chest and she gave a soft sigh of contentment when he kissed the back of her neck.

"I have not slept well since I left your bed," she confessed sleepily.

"Nor have I," he admitted. "My love, did Farlan – did he rape you?"

"No." She shook her head, wincing a little. "He did not, Traven. I swear it."

He ran a gentle finger over her swollen lip. "I will kill him for what he did to you."

"No," she murmured. "It is not worth taking a life." She muttered something else, too low for him to understand, before her breathing slowed into a deep and even rhythm.

He kissed her neck again, inhaling the soft scent of her skin before whispering, "He will beg for the mercy of death before I am finished with him."

CHAPTER 9

Elena stared at the far wall of Traven's bedroom. She was sitting up in his bed, pillows piled behind her back and the sheets tucked around her. It had been four days since Farlan attacked her and she was annoyed at how weak and tired she still was. Aldina had helped her bathe and washed her hair earlier and it had awakened the pain in both her shoulder and side.

Plus, she had seen her face for the first time since the attack and she was horrified by her black eye and swollen face. She rolled her eyes and blew her hair back from her face.

Be truthful, Elena. You are horrified that he *has seen you looking this way.*

She had never considered herself particularly vain, but the thought that Traven had seen her looking so terrible was making her face hot with embarrassment.

She needed to get over it. It would not do to forget that the moment she took his collar off, Traven refused to speak to her. He was being kind now only in the hopes that she would wear his collar again. It was better that she looked so awful. It would cool his desire for her and make him less eager to claim her for his own.

But, would that be so bad? You enjoy his touch and he is kind enough to you. You wore his collar for a week, and it did not kill you to do so. You did not even notice it after the first day. There would be no more men touching you, pursuing you, or trapping you in a stable and beating you. Despite how you feel about the collar, he is right in that it will keep you safe when you are not with him.

Elena closed her eyes. What she was thinking was ridiculous. She could accept Traven's collar, wear it around her neck and share his bed but when he tired of her, what then? He could claim that he would not tire of her, but his reputation suggested otherwise. She was not interested in being just another of his conquests, nor was she interested in watching him move on to another woman once he was finished with her.

She had only shared his bed for a week but already she understood too clearly why his previous lovers had chosen to leave his household when he was finished with them. If he treated them as sweetly as he treated her, and they had allowed themselves to fall in love with him...

She shifted, groaning as sharp pain shot down her arm. She was smart enough to not fall in love with him, but it did not mean she didn't care at all for him. In a few days, when she had healed a bit more, she would ask Traven to return her to her own room. The sooner she started distancing herself from him, the less it would hurt when he found another.

The door to the bedroom opened and Aldina entered, carrying a tray with a bowl of stew and a glass of milk. "It is time for lunch, Elena."

"I am not hungry," Elena replied.

Aldina shrugged. "You must try and eat anyway. You

have eaten very little in the last few days and food will help you regain your strength. Plus, you cannot have any of the pain relief the doctor left until you eat a few bites."

Elena scowled at her. "That is not fair, Aldina. You would let me be in pain just so that you can force food down my throat?"

Aldina grinned. "Aye, I would. You think me cruel, do you?"

"I know you are." Elena wrinkled her nose at her and Aldina laughed again.

"Come, my love, I know you are in pain and tired, but I will get you to eat if I have to feed you myself."

Elena sighed heavily as Aldina put the tray on her lap, "I am tired of lying in this bed, Aldina. I wish to feel the sun on my face and smell the fresh air. It is so stuffy in here. If I eat, will you help me outside for a quick walk?"

Aldina shook her head. "You have gone mad, Elena. Just helping you into the tub this morning nearly made you throw up from the pain. You cannot walk downstairs and outside. Stop being so foolish and eat your stew and drink your milk."

Elena stared stubbornly at her. "I am not hungry, and I do not like milk."

"Where is this coming from?" Aldina said. "You are usually so agreeable."

Elena blinked back the sudden, hot tears. "I do not know. I feel like I am going -"

The door opened and Traven strode through. He was dressed in a warm cloak, with a wool hat on his head and he smelled of the cold air. At the sight of his red cheeks, Elena scowled. He'd been outside enjoying the fresh air.

He sat down beside her on the bed and smiled at her. "How do you feel today, sweet Elena?"

"Fine," she said shortly.

He frowned. "You are pale."

"It was difficult and painful for her this morning when I helped her bathe," Aldina said. "And now she is refusing to eat."

Elena gave her a dirty look as Traven looked at her sternly. "You need to eat. Elena. It is the best way to regain your strength. You are too pale."

"I am pale because I have been cooped up in your bedroom for the last four days," she said peevishly.

"The last time you were in my bedroom for four days, you did not seem to find it unpleasant," he teased gently.

"Very funny, my lord." She glared at him. "Tell Aldina that she is to help me go outside and take a walk."

He bellowed laughter. "No, my love, I will not."

She was horrified to find herself close to tears and she blinked them back angrily. She already looked awful, she did not wish to make it worse by blubbering like a child.

Traven studied her closely. "Elena, are you all right?"

"I am fine," she muttered. "I would like to be alone please."

Instead of leaving, he tipped her chin up and stared at her for a long moment. She blinked rapidly, her grey eyes swimming with tears, and he gave her a kind look.

"Come, my love. If it is fresh air you want, it is fresh air you will get."

Aldina made a sound of disapproval. "My lord, I do not believe that is wise. She is very -"

"Bring me blankets, Aldina." Traven ignored her protests.

Aldina sighed and handed him blankets. Moving carefully, Traven wrapped Elena in them until only her head was exposed. He slid his arm under her legs and another around her upper body.

"Are you ready? This is going to hurt," he warned.

She nodded, and he lifted her from the bed in one smooth motion. She flinched and he paused. "Should I stop?"

"No, Traven. It only hurts a little."

He looked behind him at Aldina. "Bring the tray of food please, Aldina."

He carried her downstairs and out the door. The sun was shining brightly, and he walked a few paces into the courtyard. Elena lifted her face to the sun and breathed deeply of the fresh, cold air.

"Better?" he asked.

"Yes, thank you, Traven." She smiled gratefully at him as Bryce came scurrying into the courtyard.

"Elena!" He grinned delightedly at her and she smiled down at him.

"Hello, Bryce."

"How do you feel?"

"Better. I owe you a thank you for helping me."

He blushed and looked at the ground. "If I had a sword, I would have killed him."

"Do not say that, Bryce," she chastised.

"Run and get a chair from the kitchen, boy, and be quick about it," Traven said.

Bryce nodded and ran to the castle. He returned only a few minutes later, dragging a chair behind him. Traven set Elena carefully into the chair. He pulled the wool hat from his head and put it on hers, tucking it down past her ears.

"There. I will return in half an hour. You are to eat all of your lunch." He glanced at Aldina and Bryce. "You two stay with her. If she tires before the half hour, come and find me, boy."

Duncan stared curiously as Traven conversed with the old man in the common room. He stood and edged closer, straining to hear the conversation.

"How quickly can you make it?" Traven asked.

The old man shrugged. "Fairly quickly. My days are free as of late." He had a piece of paper in his hand and he scribbled a few more notes. "It will take me longer to make the furniture."

"That's fine," Traven said. "Thank you for your help, Martin."

"Aye, you're welcome, my lord." Martin hesitated. "My wife has skill with fabric and thread. She could make a few items for it as well, if you think your woman would like that."

Traven nodded. "She would. Give your wife my thanks."

He clapped the man on the back and Martin nodded to Duncan as he walked away.

Duncan frowned at Traven. "Why did you call Martin here?"

"I have need of something built. It is delicate and requires a steady hand. Martin is the best in the land."

"That is true. Although I did not realize he was still working."

"He is doing me a favour," Traven replied.

"May I ask what it is he is building?" Duncan asked.

Traven grinned at him. "It is a secret, Duncan. You will see soon enough."

Traven scowled as he watched Aldina walk down the stairs. The plate of food in her hand was untouched and he rose from his spot at the table and followed her into the kitchen.

"She did not eat her dinner?"

Aldina shook her head, "No, my lord. She says she is not hungry."

"What is wrong with her, Aldina?" The frustration was evident in his voice. "Her body is healing, but she grows more depressed by the day. I thought she would feel better after her trip outside this afternoon." He hesitated. "Do you think she is lying about Farlan raping her?"

"No, my lord. I do not," Aldina said. "I have spoken with her. She says she is just bored and tired of lying in bed all day. She has too much time on her hands to think about -"

She stopped suddenly and turned away, scraping the uneaten food into the garbage.

"To think about what?" Traven asked.

"Nothing, my lord. It is not my place to say." She gave him a solemn look. "She is used to being busy and active. She has worked since she was a small child."

"Aye, I know."

"She will be better once she is healed and back on her feet."

"Are you so sure about that?" he asked.

She hesitated before nodding. "I believe so, my lord."

He grunted and left the kitchen for the common room. He sat down in a chair in front of the fire, ignoring the others who still dined at the table. Duncan joined him, easing into the chair next to him, and drank his mead without speaking. When Bryce passed in front of Traven, he reached out and drew the boy closer to him and spoke into his ear.

Bryce nodded, "Aye, my lord, they are still there. I believe Jameson is taking one for his daughter and Ronan is taking two, but that still leaves the one."

Traven stood. "Take me to them."

SHE WAS SITTING UP IN HIS BED, STARING LISTLESSLY OUT THE window into the darkness, when he opened the door and stepped into the room.

"You did not eat your dinner," he said.

Without looking at him, she said, "No, my lord, I was not hungry. The stew at lunch was very filling."

He sat down on the side of the bed, arranging his cloak carefully around him. "You grow too thin, Elena. You must eat more."

She rubbed her side gently and continued to stare out the window. "I eat enough."

When he didn't reply, she glanced at him, "Will you take me outside again tomorrow, my lord?"

"Aye, if you would like that."

"I would. It was so nice to -"

She made a soft sound of surprise when Traven's cloak twitched. "Your cloak moved."

"Did it?" he asked innocently. "That seems strange."

It twitched again and she blinked up at him. "It just moved again."

He grinned at her. "How much pain medication did Aldina give you tonight, Elena?"

She scowled. "I am perfectly lucid, Traven. Your cloak did -"

She gasped as a soft mew was heard and a small, grey head poked its way free of Traven's cloak.

Its green eyes stared at her as she looked at Traven with wide eyes. "My lord?"

The tiny grey kitten clawed its way out of his cloak and landed with a soft thump on the bedcovers. It sat up and quickly licked the front of its chest, smoothing its ruffled fur, before looking around with bright eyes.

She held out one trembling hand and made a soft clicking noise with her tongue. "Here, kitty, kitty."

The kitten stared up at her but didn't move. She swept her good hand back and forth over the covers and the kitten crouched down with its butt in the air and its tiny tail swishing back and forth. After only a few seconds, it pounced on her hand and she scooped it up quickly, bringing it up to her face and rubbing her nose against the side of its cheek.

The kitten purred immediately, and she giggled before cradling it against her chest. The kitten climbed up the sheet covering her and settled into the curve of her neck, purring loudly and bathing itself. She giggled again when it licked her skin with its rough tongue and then chewed on her hair.

"She is so friendly." She gave Traven a look of pure glee.

"It is a boy, and yes he is very friendly. Usually the cats born in the stable are feral, but your young friend Bryce stumbled upon this litter when they were only a few days old and has been playing with and handling them ever since."

"What is his name?" She reached up and stroked the kitten's soft fur.

"That is for you to decide, sweet Elena. He is for you."

Her mouth dropped open and she stared at him. "For me?"

"Aye."

"He is so small. Is he old enough to leave his mama?" she asked doubtfully.

He smiled at her. "Aye, he is old enough. He is the runt of the litter. It is why he is so tiny. There was a bigger orange one, but Jameson had already laid claim to that one for his daughter. I am sorry."

She shook her head. "Do not be. This one is perfect."

"What will you name him?"

"Simon," she said and then gave him an anxious look. "Do you like that name?"

He nodded. "Aye, it is a fine name, my sweet."

She smiled at him and he traced first the bruising around her eye and then traced her mouth. "The swelling in your mouth has gone down."

She reached out carefully with her good hand and tugged lightly on the front of his cloak. He leaned forward so that she could brush her lips against his. "Thank you, my lord. I like him very much."

He nodded and, unable to help himself, kissed her again. She sighed and returned his kisses, opening her mouth so that he could dart his tongue between her warm lips. He groaned and slid closer, placing one big hand on her blanket-covered thigh and squeezing lightly.

She moaned and put her hand around his neck, urging him closer. He kissed down her neck and was batted in the face with a very small but very pointy paw.

"Ouch," he muttered, pulling his head back and glaring at the kitten.

It gave him an impudent look before settling once more into the curve of her neck.

She giggled. "He is only playing, my lord."

He arched his eyebrow at her. "I believe the little beast is already jealous."

She smiled and reached up to stroke the kitten. It purred and she made the clicking noise with her tongue again. It rubbed against her jaw, before kneading at her bare shoulder. She winced and Traven plucked the kitten from her and held it in one large hand.

"He is going to be a trouble maker, I can already tell," he said.

She reached for the kitten, flinching at the pain. "Can he not stay with me tonight?"

"Aye, but let's get you settled into the bed first." He set Simon down on the floor of his bedroom and she watched with amusement as the kitten chased the flickering shadows from the firelight.

"Will you stay with me as well?" Elena asked. "I know it is still early."

"Aye, I will stay with you." He hoped fervently she never realized that he could deny her nothing she asked of him.

CHAPTER 10

"Look at you!" Aldina smiled as Elena walked carefully across Traven's bedroom. "Only a week and you are already moving about."

She let out a soft gasp as Simon streaked out from under the bed and pounced on her leg before racing away. "Ouch! That rotten kitten!" Aldina rubbed her leg. "I never thought I would see the day that lord Traven would allow a cat in his bedroom."

Elena laughed, thinking about last night when Simon had pounced on Traven's head in the middle of the night, digging his tiny claws into his scalp. Traven had nearly fallen out of bed, cursing and muttering and threatening to turn the kitten into a rug. Simon had leaped off the bed and thundered across the room, promptly getting stuck under the bureau. He had mewed pitifully until Traven had crawled under the bureau and retrieved him. Both Traven and the kitten returned to the bed covered in dust, and Elena had laughed until her bruised ribs were throbbing, and her shoulder was aching.

"You seem much happier," Aldina said.

Elena sat carefully on a chair in front of the fire and

Aldina braided her long hair for her as she said, "Aye, I am more content."

It was true. Not only did Simon keep her amused, but Traven had sent Danai to his room every morning for the past three days. She had begun the job of teaching Elena to read and write, and Elena was a quick and eager student.

She glanced behind her. Traven's bedroom window faced the courtyard and, faintly, through the thick stone walls of the castle, she could hear shouts and cheers.

She faced forward and rubbed lightly at her shoulder. Today was the first day she did not have to wear the sling and although her shoulder ached, she was happy to have her arm free again.

"Where is the lord Traven?" she asked Aldina. "I have not seen him since lunch, and it is almost dinner now. It is unlike him to not stop in and see me in the afternoon."

Aldina paused for so long that Elena turned carefully to look at her. "Aldina, what is wrong?"

The older woman's face was pale, and she was giving Elena a nervous look. "Nothing, Elena."

"Is Traven hurt?" Elena asked in alarm.

"No, no. He is perfectly fine, do not worry. I believe he just had some matters to attend to this afternoon."

Behind them there were more cheers and what sounded like a scream of pain.

"What is going on in the courtyard?"

"I – I do not know." Aldina was avoiding looking at her, and Elena stood and walked slowly towards the window.

"Elena, please come back and sit down. Please," Aldina pleaded.

Elena ignored her and peered down into the courtyard. She gasped loudly and spun around, staring in horror at Aldina.

"Elena, come away from the window. You do not need to see this," Aldina begged.

"They found him." She started toward the door. "Aldina, help me down the stairs."

"What? No, Elena! You cannot leave the bedroom. You are not healed enough to -"

"Aldina, help me down the stairs or I will go down them myself and damn the consequences. I need to get to the courtyard," Elena said.

Aldina, wringing her hands nervously, followed Elena to the door. She watched as Elena paused at the small table by the door, picked up an item and then opened the door carefully. Aldina grabbed one of Traven's cloaks and followed her into the hallway.

THE CROWD GATHERED IN THE COURTYARD CHEERED raucously when the man shrieked with pain. He was strung between four men on horses, his body sagging to the ground. The ropes tied around his limbs tightened when Traven nodded, and the four men urged their horses forward again.

He shrieked, the sound echoing through the courtyard as he was lifted from the ground, his back bowing and his body stretching out to an almost impossible length as the horses danced forward.

"Mercy, my lord! Mercy!" The man screamed.

Duncan, standing next to the silent Traven, winced as blood appeared around the man's wrists and ankles. The ropes had torn the flesh wide open, and his blood spattered down onto the dirty cobblestones as the man shrieked again with agony.

"Traven, perhaps we should -"

"I will show him no mercy, Duncan. Do not ask me to do so." Traven's voice was as cold as the north wind that blew off the lake.

"Then end his life and be done with it," Duncan replied. "Do not continue this torture."

"He deserves it," Traven replied.

Traven nodded to the four horsemen again. Before they could move their horses forward, a voice called out above the jeers of the crowd.

"Traven, please stop!"

Traven held up his hand and the men reined in their horses, letting Farlan fall limply to the hard stones as Elena hobbled slowly through the crowd. She was wearing his cloak over her nightdress, and her face was pale and strained looking. She held her injured arm tightly against her side and her other hand was tucked inside the cloak. Aldina hovered next to her, her own face pale and sick looking.

As Elena passed Farlan she looked down at him. Traven could see the way her throat worked as she swallowed hard. Farlan was wearing only a pair of pants and fresh bruises were visible on his chest and torso. His face had been beaten until it was nearly unrecognizable, and the flesh around his wrists and ankles was torn wide open.

The crowd stared silently as Elena approached him. She stood in front of him, looking very small and vulnerable in front of his large body. Her breath plumed out like smoke and she shook lightly from the cold. Without speaking, she reached up and cupped his face, urging his head down toward her. Her touch sent small shivers of pleasure down his spine. He bent and she put her mouth to his ear, speaking quietly as she rubbed her hand gently across the dark shadow on his jaw.

After a moment, he raised his head and stared down at

her, his eyes dark and unreadable. She smiled tentatively at him and withdrew the plain, leather collar from within his cloak.

She pressed it into his hand and then turned around, wincing a little as she raised her hand and lifted the heavy braid of her hair away from her neck. He hesitated, and then slipped the collar around her neck, buckling it quickly before placing a soft kiss on the back of her neck.

She gave him another anxious smile, but he only stared gravely at her before taking her hand and leading her to the man lying on the ground.

When they were standing next to Farlan, Traven raised Elena's hand to his mouth and kissed it softly before dropping it. He knelt next to the moaning, shivering man. "Look at me, you stupid goat."

Farlan squinted up at him through eyes reduced to tiny slits by the swelling on his face.

Traven stared at him, breathing heavily through his nose. "It was my intention to end this day with your head on a spike atop the walls of my home. Do you see the truth of this in my face?"

Farlan moaned and nodded.

"This woman standing before you, the woman you showed no mercy to, has asked me to grant mercy to you. She has struck a bargain with me for your pathetic, worthless life. It is because of her, and only her, that you will see the sun rise tomorrow. You owe her your life." He yanked on the man's sweat-soaked hair and Farlan cried out with pain.

"Thank her," Traven snarled.

Farlan squinted at Elena with haunted eyes and whispered, "Thank you, my lady."

"Louder." Traven yanked on his hair again, and Farlan screamed thinly.

"Thank you, my lady, for your mercy!"

"I would give you counsel now, and you would be wise to heed it," Traven said in a low voice. "You are to leave my home and my lands and never return. If I even catch a glimpse of you outside of my home, I will not hesitate to cut your throat. No amount of pleading or bargaining from her will save your life again. Do you understand this, you miserable excuse for a man?"

Farlan nodded, and Traven pulled viciously on his hair before roaring, "Do you?"

"Aye, my lord! I understand!" Farlan shrieked.

Traven released him and Elena winced when his head hit the ground with a loud thud. Traven turned to Duncan. "Tend to his wounds this evening and dump him outside the walls in the morning."

Duncan nodded, and Traven carefully picked up Elena. As the crowd watched, he carried her across the courtyard and disappeared into the castle.

TRAVEN SET HER DOWN CAREFULLY ON THE EDGE OF HIS BED. He removed his cloak and knelt on the floor between her legs. He traced the collar around her neck before taking her cold hands in his own.

"You should not have gone down the stairs. You are still healing," he chastised her gently.

"It was fine. Aldina helped me."

He frowned and lifted her hands to his mouth before kissing them gently. "Still, I would -"

She gasped softly and traced her fingers over his scraped and swollen knuckles. "My lord – you are hurt. How did you…"

Her stomach clenched, and dismay flooded through her. "His face," she whispered, "you did that to him."

She dropped his hands, and he reached out to cup her face. Without meaning to, she recoiled slightly. The wounded look on his face made regret and shame course through her.

She stared at him, her eyes huge and her mouth trembling as he said, "Elena, do not look at me like that. He hurt you. He would have raped you. I could not let him go unpunished."

When she didn't reply, he cursed under his breath and stood up. He left his bedroom, slamming the door behind him as Elena buried her face in her trembling hands.

"HE IS AVOIDING ME ALDINA," ELENA SAID MISERABLY AS Aldina helped her from the tub.

"I believe he has been very busy the last few days," Aldina said.

"You are a terrible liar, Aldina." Elena sat in front of the fire.

Aldina toweled her hair dry, then tugged lightly at the leather collar around Elena's neck. "He has not asked you to remove his collar."

"Only because he will not even speak to me."

"He will get over his mood and join you in his bed soon enough."

Simon rubbed up against Elena's leg and she picked him up with one hand, taking comfort in his loud purring as she snuggled him against her chest.

"Perhaps he has found another's bed to keep him warm," she whispered.

Aldina shook her head. "He has not. He spends his nights

in the common room. He has been in a foul mood. Even Bryce, who had taken to following him around like a puppy, is avoiding him."

"It is my fault. I made him feel awful for what he did to Farlan." Elena looked up at Aldina. "I did not mean to, I swear it. It is just – I have no idea how to..."

Her face scrunched up with frustration. "My husband was so different from him, Aldina."

"Aye, he was," Aldina agreed as she combed the tangles from Elena's hair.

"Traven nearly killed a man because of me. William would never have resorted to that type of violence and I do not know how to deal with this side of Traven."

She hit her leg in exasperation, making Simon jump and skitter from her lap. "I am so confused, Aldina," she nearly wailed. "Part of me is horrified by what he did, and another part of me is – is happy and flattered by how far he will go to protect me. "

She gave Aldina a haunted look. "There was something inside of me that was delighted to see Farlan beaten so badly. What does that say about me? I am a horrible person."

"Elena it does not -"

"I promised Traven I would wear his collar for a month if he spared Farlan's life."

"That was remarkably kind, considering what Farlan did to you. You are not as horrible as you believe you are," Aldina said.

Elena laughed bitterly. "Would you like to know the truth, Aldina? I did not want Farlan to die for what he did, but I was grateful that Traven was going to kill him. It gave me a reason to bargain with him, to agree to wear his collar for longer without him knowing that I have been aching to have it back around my neck. I would not wear a collar for my sweet William, but I am desperate to wear Traven's. What is wrong with me?"

Now the tears fell and Aldina squatted in front of her, wiping gently at her wet cheeks. "Oh, Elena, you have fallen in love with lord Traven. I warned you not to do that, child."

"I could not help it," she sobbed.

Aldina gathered her into a hug and kissed her wet cheek. "And when he is finished with you, my love? What will you do then?"

Elena sighed. "I will leave his household, like all the other women before me. I will not watch him take another to his bed."

Aldina rocked her back and forth as Elena stared into the fire. "If he does not ask for his collar back sooner, I will have a month with him. He rarely keeps a woman for longer than a month, is that not right, Aldina?"

"Aye, that is right," Aldina replied glumly.

"When that month is done, when he no longer desires me, I will look for employment elsewhere."

"Elena, it is not that easy."

"It is," she insisted, wiping at her wet cheeks. "If I cannot find work, I will speak with my uncle. He may be willing to take me back into his household. It is only a half day's ride from here. You must promise to ask David to bring you to visit me. I will miss you."

"I will miss you as well, Elena." Aldina wiped away her own tears.

CHAPTER 11

Elena descended the stairs carefully. Although her bruised ribs were healed, her shoulder still ached and throbbed if she moved too quickly. She took a deep breath and moved down the dark hallway toward the common room. It was late and the castle was dark and quiet. She had lain in Traven's bed, waiting and hoping anxiously that he would join her.

After a few hours, her depression had turned to anger. He was acting like a spoiled child. She would no longer wait in his bed and hope he would join her. She would find him and give him a choice. Either he joined her in his bed, or she would return his collar and sleep in her own bed.

She entered the common room and squinted in the dim light. After a moment her eyes adjusted, and she could see his large body sprawled in a chair in front of the fire.

She moved to his side and stared irritably at him. "My lord, you are being ridiculous. Either come back to -"

She sucked in her breath when he looked up at her. His normally tanned face was pale, and his eyes were bloodshot and rimmed in red. He raised his hand and scrubbed wearily at his jaw before looking back into the fire.

"You should not be down here. Go back to my bed, girl, and be quick about it."

He grunted in surprise when she slid onto his lap and cupped his face, staring worriedly at him. "Traven, are you ill?"

TRAVEN WAS TRYING AND FAILING MISERABLY TO NOT NOTICE the way Elena's nipples were visible through the thin material of her night dress.

"Traven?" She squeezed his face. "Tell me, are you ill?"

"No. Go back to my bed," he repeated.

"I will not," she replied.

He looked at her angrily and she bit her lip. "It is cold in your bed without you. Will you not join me?"

He just snorted in reply, and she sighed before reaching for the buckle of the collar around her neck.

"What are you doing? We had a bargain remember?" His voice was testy, tired, temperamental.

"Aye, my lord, I remember. But it would seem you have tired of me and I will not force you to hold to your end of the bargain for a month, not when there are so many others willing to take my place."

He pulled her hands away from the collar. "You will use any excuse to not wear it and to avoid sharing my bed, will you not?" he said bitterly.

"Me?" Elena scowled at him. "It is you who has been avoiding me. I have spent the last two nights waiting for you to join me in your bed."

He muttered under his breath. She leaned closer, her breasts pressing against his folded arms. "What, my lord?"

"I said I will not force someone who is afraid of me to share my bed. Nor will I allow you to sleep where you are not safe or go without my collar – not after what happened. If that means I sleep here, then so be it."

She gave him a look of surprise. "Traven, I am not afraid of you."

"You are," he said harshly. "I saw it in your eyes."

She took his head in her hands again and forced him to look at her. "I am not afraid of you. I swear it. I just – I have no experience with a man like you. William would not have reacted in such a manner and -"

"And you would prefer your William's reaction." He was suddenly bitterly jealous of her love for her dead husband.

She surprised him by leaning forward and brushing her lips against his. "I would prefer to have you in the bed with me."

She rested her forehead against his. "If you have grown tired of me, my lord, I understand but then let me remove your collar and go back to my own bed. I cannot stand to be in your bed without you."

He kissed her gently. "I told you – I will never grow tired of you."

She smiled sweetly at him, but there was a look of sorrow in her eyes that he didn't understand. She ran her fingers through his hair. "When did you sleep last, my lord?"

"Two nights ago," he admitted.

She slid off his lap and held her hand out to him. "Come to bed, Traven."

He stood and took her hand, allowing her to lead him to the stairs. He scooped her up and carried her easily up the stairs and into his bedroom. He set her down and she undressed him in the dark as Simon purred and rubbed against their calves.

He climbed into the bed, sighing wearily as she slipped in next to him and put her arms around him. He wrapped his body around her like a vine and buried his face in the curve of her neck.

"Am I hurting your shoulder?" he mumbled sleepily.

"No," she whispered as Simon crawled on top of them and wedged his warm, purring body between theirs. "Go to sleep now, my love."

HE WOKE JUST BEFORE DAWN WHEN THE KITTEN STARTED kneading his arm. He gave it a gentle push off the bed. Elena had turned while he was sleeping and she was lying with her back to him, one arm curled under the pillow and the other tucked against her body.

He stared down at her, watching her chest rise and fall with deep, even breaths, and staring at the curve of her firm breasts just peeking out from the top of her night dress. He was growing hard, his erection pushing against her soft ass, and he inhaled sharply when she moaned in her sleep and pushed herself more firmly against him.

He reached out with a slightly shaking hand and tugged the loose neckline of her night dress down. Her breasts popped free, the nipples hardening slightly in the cool air and he groaned before cupping her left one. He tugged on her nipple, pulling it and rolling it between his fingers as it hardened and lengthened, and she moaned again before arching her back.

He reached down and pulled her night dress up, exposing her round and curvy ass. He nestled his hard cock between her ass cheeks and cupped her breasts again. She sighed and her eyelids fluttered open.

"Traven." She smiled and turned her head. He kissed her deeply, stroking her tongue with his and kneading her breasts gently as she arched her back. He slipped his hand between her thighs, groaning at how wet she already was.

"I have missed you," she breathed into his mouth before licking at his lips.

"Aye, I can tell how much you have missed me." He grinned down at her, chuckling when she blushed. He helped her out of her night dress, dropping it to the floor beside the bed.

"I have missed you as well, sweet Elena." He pushed her onto her back. She gave a short cry of pain, her hand reaching up to cup her shoulder and he stopped immediately. He laid back on the bed, grimly ignoring his throbbing cock and stared up at the ceiling.

She sat up and leaned over him. "Traven? Why do you stop?"

"We cannot do this, Elena," he replied.

"Yes, we can." She traced one hand across his flat abdomen and slipped it under the sheet. He moaned as she took him in her hand and stroked him firmly.

"Stop that," he muttered.

"Stop what? This?" She rubbed her thumb over the tip of his cock, and he moaned again.

"Or maybe this?" She moved her hand down his cock, squeezing at the base and twisting her fingers lightly. He shuddered with pleasure, his hips pushing into her hand. She stroked him harder and faster and as he twisted and panted beneath her hand, she leaned down, her hair tickling his ribs and kissed her way across his chest. She stopped and with a small grin, bit lightly on his flat nipple.

He growled and in one swift movement, sat up and flipped her onto her back. She cried out a little at the pain in her shoulder and his face paled. He shook his head and sat up, the sheet and quilt pooling around his waist. "This is why we cannot, Elena."

She sat up beside him, leaning against his bare arm. "Why? My shoulder will be fine."

"It will not be. I have already hurt you twice."

She rolled her eyes, "You did not hurt me, Traven."

He scowled. "I did."

"We will just go slowly." She lowered her voice to a whisper and kissed his throat, sucking gently on the skin.

"Slow?" he moaned as she licked her way to his earlobe and teased it with her lips.

"Very slow," she breathed into his ear. He turned his head and captured her mouth in a kiss.

"Promise me you will tell me if I am hurting you," he rasped out between kisses.

She ran her tongue across his lower lip. "I promise." She took his hand and sucked gently on his thumb.

"Elena," he moaned. He cupped her breast in his hand, pulling and tugging on her nipple as she shifted until she was sitting in his lap. She hooked her legs around his back and crossed her feet. She could feel his erection against her, and she arched her hips delicately against him as he gripped her bare bottom in his hands and squeezed.

They kissed again, tongues tangling together before he pulled her head back and kissed his way down her throat. She shivered as the stubble on his face scraped across the delicate skin of her throat and his hands stroked her bare back. He traced her collarbone with his tongue while his hands moved around to her front and cupped and squeezed her breasts.

She arched her back, pulling his head down to her breast.

He took her nipple into his mouth, pulling gently on it with his lips and teeth. She whimpered and moaned, running her fingers through his hair and clutching his head as he teased first one breast and then the other.

When he reached between them and ran one finger over her clit, she bucked against him. A small gasp of pain escaped her mouth. He tensed, but when he tried to withdraw his hand, she grabbed his wrist.

"No," she whispered, "make me come, Traven. Please."

He moaned into her ear. "I am hurting you. I know I am."

She shook her head. "Touch me - nice and slow." She guided his hand back to her warmth and her wetness.

He nipped her earlobe as his fingers found her small pink nub and rubbed in slow, small circles. She gasped and moaned, arching her hips into his hand as the pleasure grew within her. His fingers kept a slow, steady rhythm and soon she was panting and digging her hands into his shoulders.

"Please, my lord," she moaned.

"You said slowly, remember? Nice and slow, that is what you said," he teased.

"Oh please," she whimpered. She arched her back and her feet braced her body against the bed as she tilted her pelvis toward him. She tried to urge him to move faster with small moans of need and thrusts of her hips, but he ignored her and continued the same slow pace with his fingers.

ELENA SIGHED WITH PLEASURE. LIQUID HEAT WAS POOLING IN her belly, the coil of tension was almost more than she could bear and still Traven continued his relentless steady rhythm. He dipped his head and pulled on one hardened nipple with his teeth and that was all it took. At the feel of his teeth, the release she was looking for rushed through her and she cried out as her orgasm roared through her.

She collapsed against him, shuddering and panting. She pushed her face into his throat, licking the skin there lightly. It tasted salty from his sweat and she trailed her tongue down his neck and across his shoulder.

He moaned a little and gripped the back of her neck, pulling her back so he could look at her. "You are so beautiful, Elena." He kissed her on the mouth, and she smiled against his lips.

She reached between them, but he caught her by the wrist. He brought her hand to his mouth and kissed the palm. "No, Elena, it is enough for now."

She frowned at him. "Do not tell me what to do, Traven."

He laughed a little. "I am just looking out for you, my sweet Elena."

She sighed and he grinned with satisfaction when she started to shift her body off him. He placed his hands on her hips to help her to her side of the bed, when she suddenly threw her weight against him, knocking him flat on his back on the bed. She straddled his hips, giving him her own grin of satisfaction as she rocked gently against his throbbing cock.

He gasped when he felt her wetness against him. "You do not play fair," he moaned.

She leaned over him and placed warm, wet kisses across his chest. He groaned and grabbed her hips, pushing her into position over him.

"Not yet," she whispered. She used her good hand to pull his hands away from her hips. "Nice and slow, remember, Traven?"

She brought his hand to her breast and he cupped the warm, pale globe, rubbing his thumb over her nipple. His touch ignited little sparks of pleasure through her body and she groaned before guiding her breast to his mouth. He sucked hard on her nipple as she sighed and rubbed her hips against him in small circular motions. She gasped when the tip of his cock rubbed over her clit. It was still sensitive from her earlier orgasm and just the lightest touch made her squirm and shudder.

She rose up and positioned herself over him. He stared up at her pleadingly as she gave him a slow, sensual grin. "Do not move, my lord."

She grasped the base of his cock in her hand and slowly lowered herself onto him. He cried out as her tight velvet warmth surrounded him. He moved his hips, but she placed her good hand on his chest.

"No," she whispered. "Do not move."

"I must," he groaned.

"No," she replied. "Stay still."

Bracing her hands on his chest, she started a slow, unrelenting rhythm. He groaned and panted beneath her as she rocked back and forth.

"Slow," she moaned as she moved almost leisurely up and down. She tightened her muscles around his shaft as she slid up and down.

"Elena," he moaned. "Do not squeeze."

She ignored him. He tightened his hands around her smooth thighs, and she could see how desperately he tried to stay still. She arched her back and cupped her breasts, teasing her nipples with her thumbs as she rode him. She let her head drop back, allowing the tendrils of her long hair to tickle his thighs.

A whispered plea escaped his lips. "Please, my love. Please."

She gave a small cat-like grin of satisfaction at his whispered moan and moved faster, bracing her hands on his chest and pushing her hips up and down. He curled his hands into fists and stared into her face. She rode him harder, searching for her own release now. He grabbed her hips in his hands and she made no protest when he moved, thrusting into her wildly.

Faintly, Elena could hear her own ragged breathing as she slid up and down Traven's cock. She was lost in a haze of pleasure and was only vaguely aware of Traven's harsh panting and the sharp sting of his fingers digging into her hips. She was starting to lose her rhythm as she rocked harder and faster against him, and the way Traven was moaning and bucking beneath her was driving her mad.

With a small cry she arched her back and came furiously as Traven echoed her cry and followed her orgasm with his own. She collapsed against him, feeling the sweaty heat of his naked body against hers and the rapid, pounding beat of his heart beneath her cheek.

Gently, he rolled over until they were facing each on their sides. He pulled her close, placed one hand on the small of her back and buried his face in her neck.

"You are mine," he whispered so quietly she could barely hear him. "Mine."

CHAPTER 12

"Elena?"

"Aye, Aldina?" Elena looked up from scrubbing the large fireplace in the kitchen. It had been two weeks since she struck her bargain with Traven, and her shoulder had healed nicely. It pained her some when she spent too much time scrubbing and cleaning but today it felt good, even after spending the last half hour scrubbing the soot from the hearth.

She wiped the sweat from her forehead, leaving a smear of soot across her milky skin, and climbed to her feet. "What is it?"

"Have you seen the silver serving platters?"

"No, are they not in the cabinet?"

Aldina shook her head. "They are not. A few of the silver serving spoons are missing as well."

"That is odd," Elena said. "Perhaps one of the others are cleaning them?"

"I have asked everyone," Aldina said. "It is like they have grown feet and walked away."

Elena laughed. "I doubt that, Aldina. Someone must have

put them in the wrong spot. Come, I will help you search for
-"

"Elena?"

Elena turned and smiled at Caryn. "Hello, Caryn. Have
you seen the silver serving platters?"

The small, plump woman shook her head. "No. Aldina
asked me earlier. Your uncle is here."

"He is?" Elena gave her a surprised look. "I did not know
he was planning a visit."

Caryn shrugged. "He is waiting for you in the common
room. He seems… impatient."

Elena laughed and dipped her dirty hands into a bucket of
water. She washed them briskly. "My uncle always seems
impatient."

Aldina held her hand out to Caryn. "Are you busy,
Caryn? Will you help me search the cupboards for the
platters?"

"Aye, I can."

Elena wiped her hands dry and headed into the common
room. Her uncle was standing at the window, his hands
folded behind his back, and his foot tapping steadily on the
floor."

"Uncle Darius?"

The man turned and nodded to her. "Hello, Elena."

She paused awkwardly and then kissed him on the cheek.
"How are you, Uncle? It is good to see you. It has been too
many months since your last visit."

"Aye, I suppose it has been."

"Did you send word beforehand that you were coming?"

Her uncle arched his eyebrow at her. "Did I need to?
Have you suddenly found yourself too busy for your family?
We are, remember, the only family you have now that your
William is dead."

Elena shook her head. "Of course not, Uncle. I was just surprised to see you. I am glad you stopped by for a visit."

"Yes, well I decided it was time to visit my only niece. I heard a rumour that your master, the lord Enderson, had returned from the war. Is it true?"

"Aye."

"Good, I wish to speak to him about a business matter."

He turned and stared out the window again as Elena said, "How is Aunt Marna?"

"Doing poorly, I am afraid. Her back has been bothering her."

"I am sorry to hear that. Please give her my sympathy and my love," Elena replied.

"You can do so yourself, child. Your aunt is -"

There was shrill giggling from the hallway outside of the common room. Elena turned to see Traven enter the room. Her aunt and her cousin were hanging from his arms and he gave them both a polite smile as Elena blinked in surprise.

"Elena!" Her aunt smiled stiffly at her and crossed the room. Elena went to hug her, and her aunt stepped back, a grimace of disgust crossing her face. "You are filthy. What-ever have you been up to?"

Elena stared down at herself, feeling a hot blush rise in her cheeks. Her apron and dress were covered in soot and despite washing her hands, there was dirt embedded in her knuckles and under her nails.

"Sorry, Aunt Marna. I was cleaning the fireplace in the kitchen."

Her aunt sniffed. "I see. You have soot on your forehead."

Elena blushed again as she glanced around her aunt. "Hello, Sephina. It is good to see you. It has been a few years."

Her cousin ignored her. She was staring up at Traven, and

Elena swallowed down her jealousy when she pressed herself against his arm. "Lord Traven, my cousin did not tell me how handsome you were." She smiled at him and rubbed her hand over the hard muscles of his upper arm.

Traven smiled politely and raised her hand to his mouth. He kissed her knuckles and then dropped her hand and stepped back. "I assure you – I was much prettier before the war."

Sephina laughed, the sound too shrill and too loud. "Believe me, my lord, you are very pleasing to the eye – battle scars and all."

"Thank you, Sephina." Traven took another step back as the blonde-haired beauty moved toward him. "I imagine you would like to say hello to your cousin."

"What? Oh, of course." Sephina gave him another bright smile and turned to face Elena.

"Elena, it is so good to…"

Her voice dwindled to a stop, her mouth dropping open as she stepped forward and peered at Elena's neck. "Is that a collar around your neck, cousin?"

Elena touched the collar around her neck. She had forgotten about it. She'd grown accustomed to its weight around her neck and it, surprisingly, felt almost natural to be wearing it. Her cheeks burned as her cousin burst into loud laughter.

"I cannot believe it! You, of all people, with a collar around your neck!" Sephina squeezed Elena's red cheek in a cruel pinch. "You were always so snobby about wearing a collar. Not even your poor dead William could get you to wear one."

She turned to her father. "Daddy! Do you see Elena wearing a collar? Do you remember how she turned up her nose at the women who wore collars at our home?"

"Aye, I remember." Her uncle held her chin and lifted it up so he and Sephina could examine the collar closely.

"It is so ugly and plain." Sephina wrinkled her nose. "I would be ashamed to wear it around my neck. Who does it belong to, cousin?"

Before Elena could reply, her uncle said, "Most likely another common blacksmith or servant in lord Enderson's home. A widow like yourself cannot have many prospects, I would imagine."

He squeezed Elena's chin. "Tell me who it is, Elena. Who has managed to convince you to part your legs and wear their collar?"

Elena, her nostrils flaring and her eyes flashing fire, shook her head. "That is none of your concern, Uncle."

Her uncle frowned and Elena gasped when his fingers dug into her flesh. "You will tell me what I want to know, Elena. I will not tolerate your disobedience. Now, tell us who you have whored yourself out to right this instant or I will -"

Sephina squealed with alarm, and Elena stumbled back when her uncle was yanked away from her. Traven, his face an alarming shade of red and his eyes darkened to jade with anger, shoved her uncle against the wall.

Darius made a sharp cry of fear as Traven wrapped his large hand around the older man's neck and glared at him. "The collar belongs to me. And you would be wise, old man, to hold your tongue around me lest I rip it from your mouth."

"Forgive me, lord Enderson. I did not mean to insult you," Darius said quickly.

"I know exactly what you meant to do," Traven growled as Elena approached them and placed her hand on his arm.

"Please, my lord," she said. "My uncle can be gruff, but I assure you, he loves me."

"I do." Darius cleared his throat. "She is like a daughter to me."

Traven snorted and released the man before putting his arm around Elena's waist. He drew her close to his body and gave her uncle a stony look. "Your wife and daughter tell me you have plans to stay a few days."

"Aye," Darius said.

"For what reason?"

"To visit with my niece. It has been many months since we saw her last and her cousin has missed her." He glanced at Sephina who gave Traven a nervous nod.

Traven stared silently at the man for a moment. "You are welcome to stay in my home so that Elena may visit with you. But if I hear another unkind word from your mouth about her, I will remove you from my lands and there will be no invitation to return. Is that clear?"

"Aye," Darius said.

Traven glanced down at Elena. "You may take the next few days off from your work to visit with your family."

"Thank you, my lord. That is very kind of you." Elena could feel the anger rolling off of Traven in slow waves and his big body was tense. She stroked his back soothingly, trying to ease his anger.

He grunted in reply and then glanced at her family. "Dinner will be served in an hour or so. I imagine you are tired and would like to rest from your journey. Elena will show you to your rooms."

His gaze returned to her. "Come to my room when you are finished showing your family to their rooms."

"Aye, my lord," Elena replied.

He gave her uncle another grim look. "Remember, old man. Hold your tongue."

He stalked out of the room, and Elena smiled at her family. "Come, I will show you to your rooms."

———

"Traven?" Elena's voice drifted out of the darkness.

"Hmm?" He rubbed her lower back, their legs tangled together as Simon sat on Elena's hip, purring loudly. Their lovemaking had ended almost an hour ago and he thought she had fallen asleep.

"Thank you for letting my family stay for a few days. That is very kind of you."

He could feel his anger brewing at just the mention of her despicable family. Elena pressed a kiss against his chest. "Your anger warms the entire bed, my lord."

He grunted. "Your family is terrible, Elena."

"They are not," she said. "They are perhaps not as kind as some, but they are not terrible. Remember, they could have -"

"Aye, I know," he said irritably, "they could have abandoned you. In some ways, what they have done is worse. They make you feel beholden to them. That is not love, Elena."

She sighed. "I do not wish to fight, Traven."

"We are not fighting. We are discussing the wretchedness of your family."

She giggled and despite his anger, he couldn't help but smile at the sound. He loved her laugh.

"You are being dramatic again, but I will forgive you since you made me come three times tonight," she said teasingly.

He cupped her ass and gave it a squeeze. "Are you looking for another, sweet Elena?"

She kissed his chest again. "Your appetite is insatiable."

"It is," he agreed. "How long is your family staying?"

"I do not know." She hesitated and then said, "My uncle is not here just to see me."

"Aye, I figured as much."

"He says he has a business matter to speak to you about."

"Does he? What business?"

"I do not know," she said. "Will you at least speak with him about it?"

He made a non-committal grunt and she rubbed his chest. "Please, Traven? They are my only family and -"

"They are not your only family," he said. "You could be…"

"I could be what?" She asked.

"You could be with child." He reached down and stroked her flat belly.

He wondered if she could hear the excitement in his voice. Until Elena, he had always pulled out before his release, had never once let himself come inside a woman he fucked. At first, he had decided his reluctance to pull out came from not being with a woman for so long. Their first night together in the cave, he hadn't given a single thought to not coming inside of Elena.

But that excuse could only work for so long and now he had to admit to himself that he was doing it on purpose. If Elena carried his child, she would have no choice but to stay with him. No choice but to spend every night in his bed, her belly round with his baby and his collar securely around her neck. She would be his forever and he would no longer be kept awake at night by thoughts that she would leave him when their latest bargain ended.

She hadn't said anything, and he stroked her belly again. "Did you hear me, Elena?"

"Aye," she said. "I take the tea, my lord."

Disappointment, as bitter and foul as one of Aldina's herb potions, flooded his mouth. He swallowed heavily. "Do you?"

"Aye. William and I were waiting to start a family, so I took the tea every week. You know that Aldina brews it for those women in the household who want to wait to have children. After William died, I just... I never stopped taking it. It had become a habit to sit with the others in the kitchen each week, I suppose. And drinking the tea on a regular basis helps lessen the pain during my monthlies."

He didn't – couldn't – reply. Never before had he felt such a wave of crushing disappointment and he was thankful for the thick cloak of darkness in the bedroom. He didn't realize he was squeezing Elena around the waist until she pulled at his arm.

"My lord, you hold me too tight."

"Sorry." His voice was hoarse. He rubbed her side. "Did I hurt your ribs?"

"No. Will you tell me what is wrong?"

"Nothing is wrong," he said. "But it grows late, and we should get some sleep. Good night, Elena."

"Good night, Traven."

He could hear the worry in her voice, and he pulled her close and buried his face in her neck, seeking comfort from her softness and her warmth.

"Traven, what are you looking for?" Elena laced up her shirt before joining Traven at the dresser.

He was rooting through the small wooden box that held his watch and a few other pieces of jewelry. He frowned as he pushed aside a sturdy looking silver bracelet. "Two of my rings are missing."

"Are you certain?" She peered into the box as Traven nodded.

"Aye. The one from my father is still here, but there are two that I bought from a peddler last year that are gone."

He turned to stare at Simon who was sitting on the bed, lazily licking his paw and swiping it across his face. "Did you steal them, cat?"

Elena laughed as she got down on her knees and scanned the shadowy area beneath the dresser. "What use would Simon have for your jewelry, my lord? They are not under the dresser."

She stood up. "You are positive you returned them to the box?"

"Aye," he said.

"Aldina said yesterday that two of the silver platters were missing as well as some of the serving spoons," Elena said.

Traven sighed. "It would seem we have a thief in our midst."

"It is not Bryce," Elena said quickly. "He would not steal from you, Traven."

He smiled at her and drew her into his arms before kissing the tip of her nose. "Aye, I know, Elena. Do not worry. I have some matters to take care of this morning and will not be joining you and your family for breakfast, but I will see you later. All right?"

"Aye, Traven."

He kissed her again before leaving the bedroom. She sat down on the bed next to Simon and stroked his soft fur. She'd laid awake last night, long after Traven had fallen asleep, wondering about the disappointment she'd heard in his voice after he realized there was no chance that she could be with child.

Did he want her to be carrying his child? She thought

he'd be happy to know that he didn't have to worry about a woman he was not in love with carrying his baby. Instead, his odd silence and then the obvious discontent in his voice made her spend most of the night in a state of confusion.

"Perhaps he cares more for me than I thought," she said to the cat.

Simon made a chirping noise and batted at the end of her braid. Elena smiled. "Aye, I know. It is just wishful thinking on my part." She picked up the cat and kissed his head. "Come, little one. It is time for your breakfast, but then you must return to the bedroom rather than play in the common room like you normally do. I would not be surprised if Sephina demanded me to give you to her the moment she laid eyes on your handsome face."

"Is the lord Enderson's household always this... busy?" Her aunt had to raise her voice to be heard over the sound of the others in the common room.

There were about half a dozen servants in the room, talking amongst themselves as they cleaned. Duncan and a few of the other men were sitting at the large table, discussing plans for the crops they would plant in the spring, and Danai was in her normal spot close to the fire. As usual, almost a dozen children had gathered around her, shrieking and giggling as they took turns playing with their toys and climbing into Danai's lap.

"Lord Traven's estate is large," Elena said, "and all who live here are welcome to be in the common room."

Her aunt sniffed loudly and tucked her skirt in as a servant walked by. "He would do well to consider not allowing so many to take advantage of his compassionate nature."

Elena wanted to laugh. Traven was a good man, but compassionate was not a word that sprang to mind when she thought of him. Of course, her aunt and uncle only ever saw what they wanted to see.

"Lord Traven believes that it his duty to take care of the people who live here," she said.

"Indeed." Her uncle stretched out his legs and brushed some lint from his pants. "Where is the lord Enderson? I thought he would join us for breakfast."

"He had some other matters to take care of." Elena turned to her cousin. "So, Sephina, how have you been?"

"Fine." Sephina studied the collar around Elena's neck. "How long have you worn Traven's collar?"

"A few weeks now," Elena replied.

"Is it serious?" Sephina asked.

Elena hesitated. It wasn't serious but she didn't want to tell Sephina that. She was being ridiculous, Traven had no interest in her cousin and that was obvious, but she still did not wish for Sephina to know she was Traven's bed warmer and nothing else.

"Have you gone mute? Answer your cousin, girl," her uncle said irritably.

"You always had the worst manners," Marna said. "I swear, I tried a thousand times to teach you proper manners, but you refused to listen." She sighed and nudged Sephina. "Not that we could expect much from a child born to a simpleton and his wife."

"My father was a good man," Elena said.

"How would you know?" Sephina asked. "You do not even remember him or your mother. Do you?"

Elena gritted her teeth and forced a smile. It was not the

first time her aunt and cousin had spoken maliciously about her parents and it would not be the last. Normally she ignored it, but today, she could feel the slow burn of anger in her belly. Traven was right, they did treat her poorly and perhaps it was time she stood up for herself.

Do not, Elena! You must not forget that in another two weeks, you will be kicked out of Traven's bed. If you cannot find employment elsewhere, you will be forced to return to your uncle's home. Do not fracture your relationship with him now.

That was true. Although, she did have a third option. She could stay in Traven's household, watch as he took another to his bed. Perhaps this woman would be his wife. Perhaps he would give her many children and they would live a full and happy life while Elena remained alone forever. Turning old and grey while she pined for a man who built his life with another.

She grimaced as anger and dismay and sorrow all bubbled together in her chest. She would rather return to her uncle's home and listen to their snide comments for the rest of her life.

"Answer me, Elena," Sephina said peevishly.

"Aye, you are right, cousin. I do not remember either of them very well."

"Obviously," Sephina said. "Now, is it serious between you and Traven?"

She wanted to lie, oh how she wanted to lie, but if Sephina asked Traven about it, he would know Elena lied. If he thought Elena wanted more, it might spook him and perhaps he would kick her out of his bed before the month was up."

"No," she said. "It is not."

"Good," Sephina said. "Daddy, I want Traven for myself."

Elena's mouth dropped open as her aunt gave Sephina a look of surprise. "Sephina, child, are you certain? You see his household, do you not?"

"Aye, I do." Sephina looked around the room with distaste. "But once we are married, I will change how the household runs."

Marna laughed. "Aye, I suppose you will. You always do get your way."

Sephina smiled at her before turning to her father. "Daddy, you must make arrangements with Traven to allow me to stay a few months with him. All right?"

"Dearest, perhaps you should think about it for a day or two," Darius replied.

"No, Daddy!" Sephina whined. "Traven is the one, I know he is."

"All right," Darius said indulgently. "I will speak to the lord Enderson about you staying when we leave."

"Thank you, Daddy," Sephina said. "Now, Elena, tell me everything there is to know about Traven. What are his likes and his dislikes?"

"I will not," Elena said.

Sephina stared at her in shock. "What did you say?"

"I said I will not. If you want Traven, you will have to win him over on your own."

Elena could hear the gasp her aunt made, even over the racket of the common room. She folded her arms tight across her torso and stared steadily at her cousin as Marna said, "How dare you speak to Sephina that way."

Elena didn't reply. She was most likely ruining any chance of returning to her uncle's household, but she suddenly didn't care. She would not help her cousin win

Traven's favour no matter the consequence.

"You will do what I tell you to do, Elena," Sephina said. "You owe me."

"Owe you? For what?" Elena said.

"You spent your childhood in my home rather than on the street, did you not?"

"Aye, because of your father. It had nothing to do with you," Elena said.

Sephina scowled at her. "If I had not wanted you there, Daddy would have kicked you out."

Elena had no doubt that was true. Before she could respond, Traven entered the common room. Sephina sprang to her feet and hurried across the room, hooking her hand into the crook of his elbow and holding out her other hand for him to kiss. "Lord Traven, I am so glad to see you."

Traven ignored her outstretched hand and Elena suppressed her grin when he tugged her hand off of his arm. "I trust you slept well last evening, Sephina?"

"I did. Although," she gave him a coquettish smile, "the bed was rather cold. Perhaps there is something you could do about it."

"I will have more blankets brought to your room," Traven replied.

"That is very kind of you, my lord," Sephina purred. "But I was thinking that there was something you personally could do to help."

Traven studied her. "I do not act as a bedwarmer for my guests. Besides, you know that it is your cousin's bed I warm. The disrespect you show Elena by asking me to fuck you, is not an attractive quality, Sephina."

Her aunt and uncle stared in silent shock as Sephina's face turned bright red. Elena clapped her hand over her mouth and manufactured a coughing fit to hide the wild spat of giggles exploding from her lips.

Never had she been as thankful for Traven's blunt manner of speaking than this moment. His words left no room for doubt as to his distaste for her cousin. She had the strongest urge to take his hand and coax him upstairs. Her need and lust for him was rocketing through her. She would take him upstairs, strip him naked, then suck his cock and fuck him in all of his favourite positions.

"Elena, do you need some water?" Traven asked.

She shook her head. "No, m'lord."

Sephina was still standing next to him, the shock written all over her pretty face. "Daddy?" She whispered. "Daddy, did you hear what he said to me?"

Elena's uncle stood and cleared his throat. "Sephina, he was right to chastise you. Forgive my daughter, lord Enderson. She is occasionally too bold."

Traven nodded as Sephina's shocked gaze turned to her white-lipped mother. Marna shook her head very slightly as Darius smiled at Traven. "Lord Enderson, I wondered if you might have a moment to speak with me in private."

Traven's gaze slid to Elena. She gave him a small smile and crossed her fingers that he would at least consider talking to her uncle. The silence stretched out like warm taffy as Traven continue to stare at her.

Finally, he said, "Aye, we can speak now. Come, we will find a quiet room."

Elena released her breath as her uncle walked toward Traven. Darius took Sephina's arm and gave her a gentle push in Elena and Marna's direction. "Go visit with your cousin, Sephina."

"Actually," Traven was staring at the doorway to the common room where an older man was standing quietly,

"Aldina needs Elena in the kitchen for a little while. She will return in an hour or so." He glanced at the old man before turning to Elena. "Go on, girl."

"Yes, m'lord." Elena walked by them, giving Traven's hand a small squeeze. He squeezed back and she smiled at the old man in the doorway as she approached him. "Hello, Martin. It has been a while since I saw you last. How are you?"

"Aye, it has been a while. I am good. How are you?"

"I am well, thank you. Did you bring Talina with you?" Elena asked.

"No. I am only here to drop off a package for lord Traven. He asked me to make him a -"

"Martin!" Traven's voice rang out. "Join me, please."

"Excuse me, Elena." Martin made a short bow before walking toward Traven. Elena glanced behind her at Traven. The look of childlike excitement on his face made her pause, and he winked at her.

"Go on, girl. I will call for you when I am finished with your uncle."

CHAPTER 13

"Well, what do you think, lord Enderson? Are you able to help me with my," Darius paused, "small problem?"

"Small problem?" Traven stretched his legs out in front of the small fireplace. "It would seem losing a large amount of your wealth is more than a small problem, lord Darius."

Darius flushed. "I told you, it was not my fault. The -"

"You have allowed your wife and your children to run your household into the ground. Perhaps you should have kept them under better control. Or, perhaps," Traven eyed Darius' flabby neck, "it is you who should be wearing a collar."

Darius' face was now nearly purple. Traven could see how difficult it was for the man to hold his tongue and he took a perverse pleasure in needling him. "Do not despair, lord Darius, you are not the first man, nor will you be the last, to be controlled by their woman."

"Will you help me or not?" For the first time, Darius' voice had lost its ingratiate quality.

Traven stared silently at him before nodding. "Aye, I will give you the loan you ask for."

Darius slumped in the chair before pulling a handkerchief from his pocket and wiping his forehead with it. "Thank you, lord Enderson. Your generosity and kindness toward my family is -"

"Make no mistake, Darius." Traven leaned forward. "I do this not for you, but for Elena. For some reason, she is under the belief that she owes you a debt." Traven's smile turned bitter. "A man who treats his own flesh and blood as a slave does not deserve my help or my mercy."

"Lord Traven, I did not -"

"Hold your tongue," Traven snapped. "Our bargain has not yet been sealed and there is still time for me to change my mind."

Darius sat back, his hands in fists on his thighs as Traven said, "The way you treated Elena as a child is despicable. You are lucky that she is kind and loves you despite your poor treatment of her. She is the only reason that you and your family are welcome in my home. She is the only reason that you will receive the money you need to keep your estate and your lands. You owe *her* a great debt. One that you would be wise to never forget. Do you understand?"

"Aye, lord Enderson, I understand."

"Good," Traven said. "Later this afternoon, the papers will be drawn up for our loan agreement. Once they are signed, you may spend another day or two visiting with Elena. After that, you will leave and not return to my home until I invite you to return. Are we clear?"

"Aye," Darius replied.

The door to the small room opened and Duncan stuck his head into the room. "Traven, do you have a moment – forgive me, I did not realize you were busy."

"Come in, Duncan. Elena's uncle and I are finished our business," Traven said.

Duncan joined them and Traven nodded to Darius. "Leave us."

Without a word, Darius stood and walked out of the room. He shut the door with a hard bang and Duncan grinned at Traven. "He seems displeased."

Traven grunted. "He is a man used to others being impressed by him."

Duncan sat in Darius' empty chair. "It is lucky that Elena does not have the same disposition as her cousin. That girl is a nightmare. She has been here only a day and already the servants hate her. I heard them gossiping about her in the kitchen earlier."

"Aye, she is unpleasant," Traven agreed. "Elena is nothing like her."

"Martin asked me to give you his apologies, but he could not stay after he delivered your package," Duncan said. "David and I helped him unpack it from the wagon."

"How does it look?" Traven asked.

"It is perhaps Martin's finest work."

"Is it in the common room?" Traven asked.

"Aye. Martin finished setting it up only five minutes ago. The children can barely keep their hands off of it. Before I left, David was attempting to herd them away from it like they were deer."

"Is Elena still in the kitchen?" Traven asked anxiously. "I want to be there when she first sees it."

"Aye, Aldina is doing a fine job of keeping her distracted," Duncan replied. "Although perhaps you should go down to the common room now and show it to her before the children break past David and claim it for their own."

Traven smiled a little. "Aye, I will. But first, tell me what is wrong."

Duncan gave him a cautious look. "Nothing is wrong."

"We have been best friends since we were children, Duncan. You have never been able to lie to me, do not attempt to do so now," Traven said.

Duncan sighed. "Truthfully, I do not know what is wrong with me. Ever since I returned from the war, I have been… unsettled."

"Aye, that is not uncommon. I felt unsettled myself. It is difficult to go from battle to your normal life again. You just need to find your routine again, Duncan, perhaps find a woman and -"

"It is more than just that," Duncan said. "I no longer feel like…"

"What?" Traven asked.

"Like I belong here."

Shock rolled through Traven as Duncan grimaced. "I know that sounds harsh, but it is like I am adrift, just a weed floating aimlessly on the lake. Nothing brings me joy or happiness. I feel like I am meant for something different, but I do not know what it is. My place is no longer here in your home, Traven."

"You mean to leave then?" Traven asked. Dismay was making his breakfast curdle in his stomach.

"Aye," Duncan said. "I believe I do."

Traven didn't say anything and after a long moment of silence, Duncan clasped his hands between his knees and leaned forward. "Are you angry with me?"

"No, of course not," Traven said. "You are my best friend, Duncan, and I will support you in whatever you choose to do. But I am asking you, as your friend, to consider your decision very carefully before you make it. Do not be hasty in believing that leaving your home will solve your discontent. All right?"

"Aye, Traven. I will think on it for a while longer," Duncan replied.

"Thank you, old friend." Traven stood and clapped him on the back. "Come, join me in the common room while I show Elena her surprise."

———

TRAVEN WAS NERVOUS. HE WAS A MAN WHO HAD SURVIVED A war, a man who was in charge of a large estate and all those who resided in it, and never before had he felt the type of anxiety he did in leading Elena to her surprise.

Duncan was walking behind them, and he knew from the grin on the man's face that he was well aware Traven was barely able to keep his breakfast down. It was foolish to be so nervous. He had no doubt that Elena would be gracious and kind when she saw it, but he realized that he wanted more than that. Selfish as it was, he wanted her to be thrilled by it, wanted her to love it desperately and realize how much she meant to him when she saw it.

Perhaps you should just tell her how much she means to you, rather than plying her with gifts and expecting her to understand what they mean.

His stomach rolled again. Telling Elena how important she was to him was an even more terrifying thought. He'd rather be back on the battlefield. He knew she cared for him, but did it go beyond that? Most likely not. From the little bit she had revealed, her dead husband was the total opposite of Traven, and it was obvious how much she had loved her husband.

Still loves him, most likely. He never forced her to wear a collar.

He grimaced. No, he had not, and if Traven truly wanted to win her over, he should tell her that she did not have to wear his collar either. But the thought of her not wearing it, knowing it would make her vulnerable, was too much for him to accept. Not when the memory of how she'd looked after Farlan went after her was still fresh in his mind. He had a feeling he would never forget it.

No, she needed to wear his collar. There would be no bargaining about that.

Then she will never truly love you.

"My lord?" Elena's soft hand gripped his as they walked toward the common room. "Are you all right?"

"Aye, why?"

"You look rather ill."

"You do look like you might vomit, Traven," Duncan said. "Perhaps you should lie down. I can get Aldina to bring her smelling salts or perhaps one of her herb potions."

Traven glared at Duncan over his shoulder. The man grinned cheekily at him as Elena squeezed Traven's hand again. "My lord, should you be lying down?"

"No," he said. "I am fine."

They were at the common room now and he stopped her before she could walk into the room. "I have a surprise for you, Elena."

"You do?" She gave him a pleased look.

"Aye. It is in the common room."

A smile crossed her face. "I love surprises."

"Close your eyes," he said.

She closed her eyes and rather than risk her stumbling, he swept her up into his arms. She giggled and slung her arms around his neck while keeping her eyes squeezed shut.

He walked into the common room and gave the children gathered around the table a gruff look. "Go on, little ones. It is not for you."

He strode toward them and they made little squeals of excitement and fear and ran back to Danai. One girl with blond braids askew and a smudge of dirt on her face – she couldn't have been more than four and so tiny, she could barely see above the table - clung defiantly to the edge of the table for a few seconds more, standing on her tiptoes to try and get a better look.

"Go on," Traven repeated.

She stuck her tongue out at him but retreated, staring longingly at the table.

Traven set Elena on her feet, only vaguely aware of the people who had gathered around them. He stood behind her and slipped his arm around her waist before kissing her soft cheek. "Open your eyes, Elena."

She opened her eyes and he felt her body tense when she saw the dollhouse. She stared at it for a long time and Traven's anxiety grew with every minute that passed.

The dollhouse stood over three feet tall, with nine rooms and a stone covered exterior. Each room was filled with exquisitely detailed furniture, there was an intricate carved staircase winding up through the three levels and small panes of glass shone in the windows. Tiny silk drapes covered the glass and there were even small dishes and platters of food made cunningly from bits of wood and clay. Duncan was right, the dollhouse just may have been Martin's finest work.

When Elena stayed silent, Traven squeezed her waist. "Do you like it?"

He could hear the worry in his voice, but Elena spun around immediately and the look on her face drove away his trepidation.

"Traven!" She flung her arms around him and pressed a hard kiss against his mouth. "I love it. It is," she paused and blinked rapidly, "it is the most wonderful gift I have ever been given. I will cherish it always."

He wiped away the tears that were spilling down her cheeks with his thumb. "I am glad you like your gift, sweet Elena."

"No," she said, "not just like. Love, Traven." The excitement in her voice was palpable. "I *love* it. I will never ever forget this day."

She turned around and stared at the dollhouse again. "Can I – I want to touch it. May I?"

He kissed her neck before unwrapping his arm from her waist. "It is yours, Elena. You may do whatever you like with it."

She rushed forward and an enormous grin crossed his face when she clapped her hands and squealed excitedly over each new thing that caught her eye. Even the others in the common room were grinning at her enthusiasm, although Traven noted that her family remained at the far end of the room with sullen looks on their faces. Aldina had come into the common room and she joined Elena, smiling at the dollhouse.

"That is beautiful, Elena."

"Aye, is it not?" Elena clapped her hands again. "It is the most beautiful dollhouse I have ever seen."

"Martin did a good job," Aldina said.

"Martin made it?" Elena turned to glance at Traven, and he nodded. "I will have to thank him the next time I see him."

"Get away now. It is not for you, little scallywags. You will break it with your chubby little fingers if you try and play with it." Aldina was shooing away the half a dozen children who had crept back in to join Elena at the table.

Elena frowned. "Of course, they may play with it. It is for everyone to enjoy."

She glanced at Traven again. "If you are agreeable to that, my lord?"

He felt a swell of pride and affection for her sweetness and her generosity, and he smiled at her. "It is yours, Elena. I meant it when I said you may do whatever you like with it."

Her face shone with happiness and he knew in that moment he would spend the rest of his life trying to make her as happy as she was right now. He watched as the children gathered around her and she picked up the little blonde girl, setting her on her hip so she could see the dollhouse.

To his surprise, the children touched the tiny furniture and the dollhouse with gentle fingers, and he grinned when Elena reached in as eagerly as they did to touch and explore. The little blonde girl scooped up the tiny cradle from the nursery and handed it to Elena before whispering something in her ear.

"Aye," Elena said, "it is small and perfect, my love."

She kissed the little girl on the cheek and smiled at her with such sweetness that his chest tightened until his heart felt like it was thumping directly against his rib cage. He had never seen Elena with a child in her arms and now that he had... his gaze dropped to her belly.

He wanted her carrying *his* child in her arms.

"YOU WANTED TO SPEAK WITH ME, TRAVEN?" GRAHAM joined him by the fire in the common room, staring with distaste at the crowd of people still gathered around the table. It wasn't just children either. "Perhaps we should go somewhere quieter."

"No need, Graham. Our conversation will not take long," Traven replied. He watched Elena as she held a tiny bureau in her hand. She was examining it carefully, her face lit up with pure joy.

"Elena seems to be pleased with your gift," Graham said.

"Aye, she does."

"Are you in love with her?" Graham's voice was blunt.

"Does it matter?" Traven asked. "Why concern yourself with something that matters little to you."

"Matters little?" Graham squeezed the arms of the chair he was sitting in. "Traven, the Ice Maiden has you wrapped around her finger. You follow her whims when it comes to issues of your lands and you think it matters little? I bore the burden of keeping your people and your lands safe while you fought a war that did not concern us. Now, because of a woman, everything I have accomplished in your absence is threatened. I know it was because of Elena that you delivered Ragnor to his death, and the old Traven would -"

"You should not speak of things you know nothing about," Traven said. "Elena had nothing to do with my decision regarding Ragnor. He was a pig of a man who raped a woman and he deserved his fate. The fact that you cannot see that makes me question your integrity, Graham. In fact, it makes me question whether I have ever truly known the real you."

Graham gave him a tight smile. "I am the same man I have always been, Traven. Just because I believe we should not be both judge and jury does not -"

"There were witnesses," Traven replied. "Now, enough. The issue with Ragnor is done and I will no longer speak of it."

"Of course," Graham said. The anger in his voice was more than clear and Traven gave him a steady look. Graham held it for a few moments before looking into the fire. "What is it you wish to speak with me about?"

"There are a number of the men you hired while I was away that I no longer wish to employ." He pulled a piece of paper from his pocket and handed it to Graham. "These are their names. You will inform them by the end of the week that their services are no longer required."

Graham shook his head. "Traven, this is over half the men I hired. Are you mad? You cannot protect your lands and your people without -"

"I charged Duncan last week with finding replacements. We will be well protected."

Graham gave him a stony look and Traven leaned forward. "Old friend, you did well in my absence. My lands and my people thrived while I was gone. But you wear blinders when it comes to the men you hired. They are no better than the thieves, murderers and rapists you hired them to protect us from. I cannot and will not allow them to stay on my lands."

"I believe you are too hasty in your judgment, Traven."

"Aye, I know you do," Traven said.

"My lord?" Elena had approached them, and Traven's cock stirred in his pants when he saw the look in her eye. "When you are finished speaking with lord Barten, will you join me in your room? There is something of importance I wish to speak to you about."

"Aye, girl. I will be along in a moment."

"Thank you, my lord." She smiled at him. It held sweet promise in it, and he ignored his urge to adjust the front of his pants. He watched the sway of her ass as she left the common room before turning his gaze back to Graham.

"We have been friends for a long time, have we not, Graham?"

"Aye," Graham said, "we have."

"I have no wish for our friendship to end over a trivial matter such as this. I am grateful for all you have done for me and you know that I love you as a brother."

Relief coursed through Traven when Graham nodded and reached out to squeeze his shoulder. "I know and I feel the same, Traven. Just know that everything I do, is for the good of you and your people."

"I know, old friend." Traven stood and headed toward the door. "I will see you at dinner."

"Aye, enjoy your Ice Maiden."

He turned, studying Graham carefully but there was no maliciousness in the man's tone or face. If Graham was still keen to make Elena his, he kept it well hidden.

Traven nodded and left the common room. He headed upstairs toward his bedroom. Graham may still want Elena for himself, but he would never have her. She belonged to him and it would be his collar and only his collar that graced her neck.

For only a short while longer.

He grimaced. Aye, the month was going by too quickly. He had to think of a way to keep Elena in his bed.

You could give her the choice to wear your collar.

For the first time in his life, he didn't immediately dismiss the idea of a woman he bedded not wearing his collar. He hated the idea, loathed it in fact, but the thought of not being with Elena was worse. Could he live with the fact that she would not wear his collar if it meant she belonged to him?

He opened the bedroom door and stepped inside the room, shutting the door firmly behind him. He honestly didn't know if he could allow Elena to go without his collar, but he only had two weeks to decide before…

His brain went blank and his cock went stiff.

Elena was lying on the bed completely naked. Her dark hair was unbraided, and she gave him a lazy smile before cupping one breast. "I thought I would have to start without you, my lord."

"Is that right?" His voice was hoarse as he stripped off his shirt and kicked off his boots. He yanked down his pants as she nodded.

"Aye. I have been waiting hours."

He laughed as he walked naked toward her. "At most, a few minutes, my sweet."

She reached between her parted legs and rubbed her fingers against her pussy. She showed him the slick wetness on them. "It does not feel like only a few minutes."

"Perhaps I should eat your wet pussy to make up for my late arrival." He stared hungrily at the juncture of her thighs, his mouth watering at just the thought of sliding his tongue up and down her sweet slit.

She sat up, swinging her legs over the side of the bed and parting her legs. "Actually, my lord, I have a better idea."

"Do you now, girl?" He stepped between her open legs, the head of his erect cock nearly brushing against her mouth. "What idea is that?"

She stared up at him. "I loved my gift, Traven. Thank you again."

He cupped her head, threading his fingers through her dark hair. "You are welcome, sweet Elena. I am glad you enjoyed your surprise."

She gave him a cheeky smile. "The dollhouse is even more beautiful and larger than the one Sephina had as a child. I believe my cousin may have been a little jealous when she saw it."

"Aye, perhaps." He gripped his cock, stroking it from root to tip as she licked her lips.

"Do you know what else makes her jealous, my lord?"

"What's that?" He rubbed the head of his cock against her lips, leaving a smear of precum behind that she eagerly licked away.

"That I get to suck your big cock and she does not," she said with a soft moan.

He smiled, his hand tightening in her hair until she couldn't move. "Aye, I believe you are right, my sweet. Open."

She opened her mouth and he slid his cock between her lips, groaning at the wet heat as she closed her mouth around him. Her tongue laved the bottom of his dick, her lips sucked firmly, and she kept her gaze trained on his face as he slid his cock in and out of her mouth.

"Good, sweet Elena," he groaned. "Suck harder, my love."

She sucked harder, her cheeks hollowing as he rocked his pelvis back and forth. He loved how open and willing she was when it came to sex. Loved that she gave herself over completely to him whenever she was in his bed.

His gaze fell on the collar around her neck and pride filled him. She belonged to him, the collar told the entire world she did. He reached down and traced it lightly, his finger lingering on the stitched crest of his family.

She was still sucking on his cock and he smiled down at her, before running his finger across the soft skin just above the collar. She moaned around his dick and he smiled again. His balls were tightening, and the base of his spine was starting to tingle as she worked him with her mouth.

He pulled her off his dick with a wet pop, holding her tight by the hair when she made a soft whine and tried to take his cock into her mouth again.

"On your hands and knees, Elena."

She scrambled back on the bed eagerly, turning over and propping herself up on her hands and knees before staring at him over her shoulder. "Traven, hurry."

He smoothed a hand over her firm ass and down the back of her thigh, watching the goose bumps erupt on her skin. "Do you wish for me to fuck you?"

"Aye," she moaned, "please fuck me, Traven."

He lost his tenuous grip on his control and stepped forward, kneeling on the bed behind her and pushing her thighs farther apart. He reached between her legs and rubbed her clit, smiling when she cried out and arched her back like a cat.

He loved fucking her on her hands and knees and had done so often in the last two weeks. She had learned quickly how he liked her to position herself and he watched as she lowered her upper half to the bed, pressing her flushed cheek against the bed and spreading her legs even wider.

"Good girl," he praised before rubbing her clit again. She squirmed and moaned, and he pressed his dick against her wet opening, sliding into her warmth until his pelvis pressed against her ass. Her fingers clenched in the sheets and when she tried to wiggle forward a little, he pressed on her lower back, keeping her in place.

"No, sweet Elena. Stay where you are." He rubbed her hip. "Take a deep breath, my love, and relax your little pussy."

She inhaled deeply and the sharp grip of her pussy eased around his cock. Despite how often he fucked her, she still needed a few minutes to adjust to his size when he took her in this position, and she often needed encouragement to relax.

He reached under her and rubbed her clit with a light touch as she moaned and arched her back again.

"Better?" he asked.

"Aye, my lord. Thank you."

"You are welcome, my sweet." He grasped her hips and slid in and out, keeping a steady and firm pace as he watched her ass bounce with every thrust. After a few minutes, he leaned over her and gripped both arms, pulling her up straight and resting her spine against his chest as he fucked her. He kissed her neck above the collar and pulled on her arms again until her back arched.

"You look so beautiful, Elena," he murmured.

She moaned in response, her soft body shaking with every thrust of his cock, her nipples hard as glass. He cupped her throat with his left hand, holding her tight as he cupped her breast and pinched her nipple.

She cried out and when she reached for her pussy, he gave her nipple another pinch. "No, my love. That is for me and only me."

"Please, Traven," she panted. "Please touch me."

He thrust harder, drawing out her need for a little longer as she rocked her body against him, and increasingly more desperate pleas fell from her lips. When he finally reached down and cupped her pussy, she cried out with pleasure, arching into his hand. He rubbed her swollen clit and, on the verge of his own orgasm, gave the swollen bud a soft pinch.

She cried his name as she came, her hips pumping furiously against him as he pushed in deep and let his own release wash over him. He held her steady through her orgasm, her knees were already beginning to buckle, as he pumped his seed deep into her pussy.

When he was finally spent, he eased her down to the bed before lying on his side behind her. He spooned her shaking body and kissed the back of her shoulder as she sighed happily. "That was incredible, Traven."

"Aye, for me too, Elena."

She turned her head and pressed a kiss against his mouth. "Each time is better than the last, is it not?"

"It is." He returned her kiss and she sighed happily before resting her head on the pillow.

After about ten minutes, she said, "Did you speak with my uncle?"

"Aye, I did. He asked for a loan."

She sat up and stared at him in shock. "A loan? Do you jest, Traven?"

"I do not," he said. "Your uncle's wealth has been depleted these last few years."

"How?" She wondered.

"He has allowed your aunt and your cousins to spend his money on foolish things," Traven said. "Now he is paying the consequences."

"How bad is it?" she asked.

"Bad enough that he requires a loan to keep his family and his servants fed."

He could see the worry on her face and while he loved her loyalty, he hated that the loathsome people she called family caused her stress.

"My poor uncle. He is so proud and always has been. It must have been difficult for him to ask you for a loan," she said.

He waited for her to ask him if he loaned her uncle the money. When the silence spun out, he said, "Are you not curious if I gave him his loan, Elena?"

"Aye," she admitted, "I am. But it is not my place to ask. It is your money and your decision, and I do not want you," she hesitated, "feeling obligated because I warm your bed, to give my uncle the money."

"I do not," he said.

She smiled at him. "Good."

"I agreed to loan him the money," Traven said.

Her relief was immediately obvious and the grateful way she looked at him made him feel both prideful and a little ashamed. Her uncle and his family deserved to end up as beggars on the street for how they treated Elena but making her happy had suddenly become one of Traven's most pressing desires.

She cupped his face and pressed a soft kiss against his mouth. "Thank you. You are a good man."

He shook his head. "I am not a good man, Elena."

She gave him a stubborn look and cupped his face again before resting her forehead against his. "Aye, Traven, you are."

CHAPTER 14

"My lord, do I still please you in bed?"

Graham gave the woman a slap on the ass. "You are good enough."

Bonnie studied him in the candlelight before pulling the covers up to hide their nakedness. "You seemed distant tonight."

"How long have we been fucking?" Graham asked.

Bonnie shrugged. "Nearly a year now."

"How many times do you pretend that I am Traven when you have my dick in your mouth or your pussy?"

She flushed and an angry look marred her pretty features. "How many times do you pretend I am the Ice Maiden, my lord?"

He grinned at her. "A fair question."

"Besides," Bonnie grumbled, "I hate both the lord Traven and his cold witch now."

"Do you?"

"Aye. He threw me away like a piece of trash the moment he saw her, and now she rubs it in my face every chance she gets."

"That does not seem like the Elena I know. She is kind to everyone."

Bonnie glared at him. "I am surprised, lord Graham, that you would still find her kind after she had repeatedly rejected your advances."

His hand tightened on her hip until she gasped and made a small moan of pain. "Watch your tongue, girl."

She gave him a sullen look. "I hate them both and I do not care who knows it."

"Is that why you are stealing from Traven's household?"

Her body stiffened and he shook his head when she started to ease away from him. "No, stay where you are."

"I-I do not know what you are talking about, lord Graham."

He laughed. "Do you think I am stupid, girl? I have seen you stealing items from the kitchen. It is almost as if you wish to lose a hand and be thrown from the household onto the streets."

Bonnie gave him a cunning look. "You are not the only one who knows secrets, my lord."

"What is that supposed to mean?"

"It means I know that Elena's husband did not die of illness. I was in the kitchen that night, tucked away in the pantry when you added the vial of liquid to his drink. It was not difficult to figure out that he had been poisoned when he grew ill almost immediately."

She cried out in pain when Graham pounced on her. He pushed her onto her back on the bed, one hand around her throat and the other digging into her stomach. His face only inches from hers, he said, "You would be wise to watch what you say, Bonnie. Someone as small and unremarkable as you would not be missed should you disappear."

Tears dripped down her face and she whispered. "My

lord, you misunderstand. I know why you poisoned Elena's husband and I do not judge you. I once loved Traven the way you love Elena. I would have done anything to be with him."

He squeezed a little tighter, smiling when the fear washed over her face. "Is that true, Bonnie?"

"Aye," she choked out. "It is."

He released her throat and she drew in a ragged breath, staring silently at him as he hovered over her. He leaned down and kissed away the jagged track of tears on her cheek, his smile widening when she flinched.

"Shh, little Bonnie. I would never hurt you."

"I-I know," she said.

She drew in a deep breath and smiled tentatively at him. He ran his thumb over her bottom lip. "Tell me, Bonnie, if you could, would you see Traven suffer for what he did to you?"

"Perhaps," she said.

"People grow sick and die every day. Even those who appear to be in good health. Would you not agree?"

She blinked at him before whispering, "My lord, you – you cannot poison lord Traven."

"Why not?" Graham said.

"Because he…"

Graham smiled at her before kissing the tip of her nose. "I would require your help, little Bonnie."

"I cannot," she whispered.

"You can," he said. "Traven treated you terribly. So terribly that you risk losing your hand and being cast out for stealing a few trinkets."

"I steal because I – I need extra money so that I may leave this place and never return," Bonnie said. "The others, they mock me behind my back, call me names and whisper that I was not good enough for him. That he tossed me aside because I could not please him."

"My little Bonnie," Graham said. "How terrible it is for you here."

"It is," she whispered.

"If I ran the household, you would not be tormented in such a manner."

"Even if Traven did…die, you would not get his estate, my lord. It would go to his sister."

Graham gave her a solemn look. "I have known Traven and his sister since we were small. She has no wish to take over her family's home, not when she is busy running her husband's estate. Trust me, she would be grateful if I offered to take it off her hands."

When Bonnie didn't say anything, he leaned over her and pressed a kiss against her mouth. "If the estate belonged to me, you would never want for anything again."

"You are in love with Elena," she said.

"Aye, I am, and with Traven gone, I would make her my wife. But that does not mean you would not be treated well, or that your wants and needs would not come above all of the other servants who worked in my home. And, if from time to time," he rubbed his hardening dick against her hip, "you yearned for a taste of my big dick, I would not be opposed to it even with Elena as my wife. Variety is the spice of life after all, is it not?"

She didn't say anything, and he tugged the covers down until her small breasts were exposed. He licked and sucked at her nipples until she was moaning, and her small body was arching against his.

"Will you help me, Bonnie?" He said as he cupped her pussy and rubbed her clit.

"Aye, my lord," she said. "I will."

"ELENA, WHAT ARE YOU DOING IN THE KITCHEN? TRAVEN gave you time off to spend with your family, did he not?" Aldina gave her a surprised look.

"Aye, he did," Elena said as she washed dishes. "But it's been three days now and I have had more than enough of my cousin's spoiled behaviour. I swear, she is worse now than she was as a child."

Aldina laughed. "She does seem like a little brat. Bryce had a crush on her until the first time he spoke to her. Now, he holds his nose and makes a face when she walks by him."

Elena grinned. "Bryce could use a lesson in manners, I suppose, but I find it terribly difficult to admonish him. He is too charming, even at eleven years old."

"When is your family leaving?" Aldina asked.

"Tomorrow morning. Does it make me horrible to admit that I will be truly relieved to see them go?"

"No, family can be trying at the best of times." Aldina suddenly reached out and tugged on the collar around Elena's neck. "How much longer until your bargain is over with lord Traven?"

"A week and a half," Elena replied. She dried her hands and gave Aldina a sour look. "I am already trying to think of ways to extend it."

"Does it still bother you to wear his collar?" Aldina asked.

"No," Elena said slowly. "In fact, it makes me anxious to think of taking it off."

"Perhaps you should just tell him how you feel," Aldina suggested. "Traven cares for you."

Elena frowned at her. "Since when did you have such a

change of heart, Aldina? Not two weeks ago, you scolded me for falling in love with him."

"Aye, but that was before I really paid attention to how Traven is with you. He is different around you, Elena. Different and… I believe he loves you."

Elena burst into laughter. "You have been drinking too much mead, Aldina. Traven does not love me."

"The dollhouse he gave you was beautiful. I saw Duncan paying Martin after he delivered it and the amount of money Martin was given would feed David and I for a year."

"Expensive gifts do not equal love, Aldina," Elena said.

"Perhaps not. But I have never seen lord Traven gift other women in the same manner."

Suddenly tired and feeling a little blue, Elena headed out of the kitchen.

"Where are you going?" Aldina called after her.

"I am going to take Simon out to the stables so he can explore and play for a bit. It is too cold for him outside, but the stables are warm enough."

She hurried up the stairs to Traven's bedroom. Simon did need some exercise and a change of scenery, she had been keeping him in the room to avoid Sephina seeing him. Although she knew it was stupid and that Sephina would not be allowed to take her cat, she still did not want her cousin even knowing about Simon.

Besides, she really did need a break from her family. Her aunt and uncle were in the common room and Sephina was in her room and they would not go out to the stables. Simon could chase mice and play with the other cats in the stables and she could have a visit with Bryce.

The door to Traven's bedroom was open and she frowned. She had shut it when she left, to keep Simon in the room, and she knew that Traven was in speaking with Duncan in another part of the castle. Even if he had returned to his room, he would not have left the door open when he left. He knew of her desire to keep Simon a secret from Sephina.

She slipped into the room, relief sweeping through her when she saw Simon sleeping on her pillow. There was movement to her left and her mouth dropped open. Bonnie was standing at the dresser. She was digging through the box that Traven kept his jewelry in and she held up the ring that his father had given him, studying it in the bright sunlight streaming through the window. She stuck it in the pocket of her skirt and closed the box.

"Bonnie," Elena said.

Bonnie screamed, her hand pressing against her chest as she stumbled back, her hip hitting the dresser and making the unlit candles on top of it, tumble to the floor.

"Elena, what – what are you doing in here?" Bonnie said nervously.

"That ring does not belong to you," Elena said.

"Wh-what ring?" Bonnie's hand rested against the pocket in her skirt.

Elena sighed. "Bonnie, I saw you take Traven's ring and put it in your pocket. You need to return it now."

Bonnie bit her lip before reaching into her pocket and returning the ring to the box. "Please, Elena, do not tell lord Traven."

"Did you steal the other stuff as well?" Elena asked. "Traven's two rings and the platters from the kitchen?"

"Aye," Bonnie whispered.

"Oh, Bonnie, why?" Elena said. "You know as well as I do what the punishment is for stealing."

Bonnie tucked her hands behind her back as if she believed Neilan would appear with his hatchet and chop one off. "I am selling the items for money."

"Lord Traven pays us a fair wage, Bonnie."

"Aye, he does. But not enough to…"

Not enough to what?" Elena asked.

"To leave this place!" Bonnie snapped. "I love him, Elena. I love him and every day I have to watch as he fawns over you. As he gives you expensive gifts and you wear his collar and he-he loves you in a way he will never love me. I cannot do it any longer. It torments me day and night!"

"I am sorry, Bonnie," Elena said. She could see the surprise spreading across Bonnie's face. "You are right, it is not fair, and I wish you did not struggle in such a manner. If I had to watch Traven with another, I would feel the same way. In fact, once he is finished with me, I will leave this place, rather than watch Traven build his life with another."

She walked toward Bonnie and hesitated only briefly before putting her arm around the smaller woman's shoulders. "I understand your pain. I really do."

"I am sorry," Bonnie whispered. "I – I have been blaming you for the way Traven treats me and that is not fair."

Elena gave her a squeeze. "Perhaps not, but again, it is understandable."

"Why are you being so nice to me?" Bonnie asked.

"We are not enemies, Bonnie," Elena said. "Perhaps we are not the best of friends, but I harbor no ill will toward you."

"I will lose my hand for this." Bonnie's voice was filled with fear. "I will lose my hand and be kicked out of the household and no one will hire me to work for them when I only have one hand. I will have to-to whore myself out just to survive."

Elena hesitated. There was a part of her, a part she didn't want to admit existed, that wanted to run straight to Traven and tell him what Bonnie had done. She did not want Bonnie to lose her hand and be thrown from the household, but if Traven knew of Bonnie's thievery, Elena could use it to strike another bargain to wear his collar.

She was almost certain that she could save Bonnie's hand and her place in the household, by offering to wear Traven's collar for another month or two.

But if you are wrong? Are you really willing to watch Bonnie lose her hand just because you wanted a little longer in Traven's bed? Could you live with yourself if Traven does not agree to your bargain? He only keeps women for a month… what makes you think you are anything special? You said it yourself earlier, expensive gifts do not equal love.

She sighed and made herself smile at Bonnie. "You will not. I see no need to tell Traven or anyone else, if you promise me you will no longer steal from him."

"Are – do you mean that, Elena?" Bonnie was giving her a frank look of shock.

Elena nodded. "Aye, I do. If you promise never to steal again from Traven."

"I promise," Bonnie said immediately. "I promise I will not. Thank you, Elena."

She threw her arms around her and Elena returned her hug. "You are welcome, Bonnie. Now, dry your tears and return to the kitchen. All right?"

"Aye, all right."

A flash of grey streaked by them and Elena muttered a curse. "Simon, no. Wait for me."

To her surprise, the cat skidded to a halt in the doorway of the bedroom. His back arched, his fur stood on end and he hissed at something they couldn't see. Elena glanced at Bonnie and they both hurried to the doorway.

They looked up and down the hallway, but it was empty. Elena glanced at Simon. His fur was still standing on end, but he purred when she scooped him up and nuzzled his neck. "I am going to take Simon out to the stables for a bit, Bonnie. I will see you at dinner."

"All right." Bonnie hesitated before taking Elena's hand and squeezing it. "Thank you again, Elena. I owe you a debt."

"You do not," Elena said firmly. "Just keep your word to me."

"I will," Bonnie said. "I promise."

ELENA DUMPED SIMON ON THE BED. THE CAT HAD BITS OF hay stuck in his fur and she laughed before picking them out. "You are covered in hay, Simon. I am beginning to regret that I took you to the stable."

"Elena?" There was a knock on the door frame, and she turned to see David standing in the doorway.

"Hello, David."

"Hello. Lord Traven wishes to see you in the common room."

"All right, would you tell him that I will be down in an hour or so?"

"He wishes to see you now, Elena."

She gave Simon a final pat and followed David into the hallway. She shut the door and gave him a curious look. "Is there something wrong, David?"

"I – it is not good."

She frowned and followed him down the stairs and through the halls to the common room. He stepped aside and she stared at Traven who was sitting in his normal spot by the fire. As usual, the common room was full of people and they all watched in silence as she walked toward Traven.

Bonnie was standing in front of him, her head bowed and

her slender body shaking. Lord Barten sat beside Traven and curiously, her cousin Sephina stood on the other side of Traven's chair.

Sephina gave Elena a weirdly triumphant look as Elena stopped next to Bonnie. "My lord, what is wrong?"

Her breath caught in her throat when she saw Neilan at the edge of the crowd. She put her arm around Bonnie's shoulders and the smaller woman leaned against her. Her face was soaked with tears and Elena gave her a small squeeze. "Do not cry, Bonnie. It will be all right."

"Elena."

She looked up at Traven, hating the look of betrayal on his face. "Yes, my lord?"

"Why did you not tell me that Bonnie was the thief?"

Bonnie made a little sob and Elena held her tighter. "Because Bonnie promised she would not do it again, my lord, and I believed her."

"I am the head of this estate. It is on me to decide whether a servant is remorseful and repentant."

"I know," Elena said.

"And yet you still had no plans to tell me the truth. Is that right?"

"It is," she said.

He sighed and glanced at Neilan. "I am disappointed in you, Elena."

"She did it because she wished to leave the household and required money to do so, my lord," Elena said. "Her heart was broken by another and she had no wish to watch him be with someone else. I understood her pain and commiserated with her. I chose to show mercy on her and keep her secret because Bonnie is a good person. It is not her fault that the person she loves does not love her. If I were in her place, I would not want to watch the man that I love be with another either."

Was it just her imagination or did guilt cross Traven's face? She studied him closely and when he looked away, she was positive it was guilt.

"How did you find out, my lord?" She asked.

Before he could reply, Sephina gave her a smug grin. "I overheard you and the little thief talking in Traven's bedroom. Unlike you, I am loyal and honest and knew that Traven would value those qualities. Perhaps now he is beginning to see that you are not worthy to wear his collar and warm -"

"Hold your tongue, Sephina. While I appreciate your honesty, you will not speak ill of your cousin in my presence."

"My lord, she let a thief -"

"I said, hold your tongue," Traven barked.

Sephina shut her mouth with a snap, hurt crossing her face as Traven leaned forward. "Bonnie, look at me."

She raised her gaze to Traven and made a soft whimper. "I am sorry, my lord. Truly. I should never have stolen from you, and I regret it now."

"Aye, I would regret it too if I was caught," Traven said. "You know the punishment for thievery as well as I do, Bonnie."

Bonnie made a sobbing gasp, and Elena was puzzled when Bonnie's gaze turned to the lord Barten. "My lord," Bonnie whispered. "Please."

"Do not beg me for mercy, girl," lord Barten said carelessly. "This is Traven's household to run, not mine. You have made your bed and now you will lie in it."

Bonnie turned to Elena. "Elena, when your husband -"

"Enough!" Lord Barten roared so loudly that his voice

echoed through the room. His face red, he glared at Bonnie. "You are a thief and a liar. Trust when I say that no one will believe a word that drips from your traitorous tongue."

Bonnie made another hiccupping sob as Neilan stepped forward. Traven held up his hand and stared at Elena. "Bonnie knows the rules and she will lose her hand today. Unless," he paused, "you wish to bargain on her behalf, Elena."

"One month, my lord," Elena said immediately.

A grin crossed Traven's face. "One year."

Something compelled her to keep playing the familiar game. "Three months."

"Nine months."

"Six months."

Traven studied her. "Six months of wearing my collar and you stop drinking the tea."

The silence in the room was deafening. Everyone in the room stared at her. They knew as well as she did, what Traven asked for.

Her pulse jumping, her stomach quivering, she said, "Agreed, my lord."

Traven's big body relaxed, and he gave her a heated look that made her pussy quiver and her nipples harden. He turned to Bonnie. "A bargain has been struck on your behalf. You will lose neither your hand nor your employment with me today, but if you are caught stealing again, there will be no more bargaining."

"Thank you, my lord. I will never steal again, I promise," Bonnie said.

She hugged Elena hard before whispering in her ear. "Thank you. Thank you so much."

Elena wanted to reply, but she couldn't stop staring at Traven. His need for her was obvious in the look in his eyes and when he stood and held out his hand to her, she untangled herself from Bonnie's grip and went to him.

He took her hand and ignoring everyone else, led her from the common room. They walked silently to the bedroom, Elena nearly running to keep up with Traven's long strides. The enormity of what she had just done wanted to sink in, but it was being overshadowed by her lust for Traven.

She wanted him. She needed him. When he ushered her into the bedroom and shut the door behind them, she immediately tore at his shirt, trying to pull it over his head as he fumbled with the lacings on her shirt. He growled and yanked first his own shirt off and then hers.

He pushed her up against the wall and kissed her hard, his tongue thrusting into her mouth as he shoved his pants down his legs. He pulled down her skirt as he continued to kiss her, overwhelming her with his taste and his scent.

He lifted her up and she hooked her legs around his waist, moaning happily when he pushed his cock deep into her soaking wet pussy. She wrapped her arms around his broad shoulders and held on tight as he fucked her hard and rough. His hot breath blew against her neck, his low voice moaning her name sent her spiraling toward her release almost immediately.

He thrust back and forth, pinning her against the stone wall and forcing her pussy to take every deep stroke of his cock. She cried his name, the familiar pleasure rising in her pelvis, and clutched frantically at his neck.

When her climax washed over her, she buried her face in his neck to muffle her loud shriek. His hands tightened on her ass as he shouted her name and slammed her up against the wall. He pinned her there with his big body as his cock pumped seed deep into her body.

She trembled against him and he kissed her upper chest

and neck, one hand cupping her breast and circling her hard nipple as he panted into her hair.

After a few minutes, he carried her to the bed and they both collapsed onto it. She was lying on her back and Traven placed his big hand on her stomach, rubbing slow circles on it. The rasp of the calluses against her soft skin made her stomach muscles flutter.

He leaned over and kissed her flat stomach before grinning up at her. "I cannot wait to see your belly grow big with my child, Elena."

She swallowed hard. Now that her overwhelming need for him had been sated, a new fear was stealing into her. "My lord, did you make this bargain with me because you want an heir?"

He didn't reply and she tried to remain calm. "Once I provide you with an heir, what will happen to me? I will not leave my child, Traven."

"I would never ask you do that, Elena. You will always be with our child." Traven sat up and studied her for a moment before reaching for the collar.

She batted his hands away when he tried to unbuckle it. "What are you doing, my lord?"

"You do not have to wear this," he said.

"We have an agreement. Six more months, remember?" She scowled at him.

"I know you hate wearing my collar," he said. "Our agreement still stands, but I will not force you to wear it any longer."

He reached for the buckle again and she put her hands protectively over it. "Stop it, Traven."

Now it was his turn to scowl. "I am trying to make you happy, Elena."

"Then allow me to choose for myself if I will wear your collar or not," she said.

"That is what I am trying to do." He gave her a look of exasperation.

"No, you are trying to make me not wear it," she said.

"You do not like to wear it!"

"That used to be true. Now it is not," she said.

He stared at her. "Why? What has changed your mind?"

"Love," she said.

"Love," he repeated.

"Aye, I love you," she said. "I know you do not feel the same way as I do, but I will not hide it a moment longer. I love you, Traven. I love you and that is why I want to wear your collar and carry your child."

He stared at her, and while she didn't regret finally telling him the truth, she hated that she couldn't read the look in his eyes. Finally, he cleared his throat and said, "You never asked me why I agreed to give your uncle the money he needs. Are you not curious why I would give it to him when it is obvious how much I hate him and his loathsome family?"

This was not going the way she hoped it would, but she would not feel sorry for herself. She had told Traven how she felt and while he did not feel the same, he had promised her he would not take her from her child, and she knew he meant it.

"I did wonder," she said. "But your money and what you do with it is none of my business."

He cupped her face. "It is, Elena. Everything about me belongs to you. My money, my home, my lands, my heart… it is irrevocably and forever yours."

"Traven," she whispered as joy washed over her.

He pressed a kiss against her lips. "I gave your uncle the money because he is your family and while I may not like them, I love *you* and I will always take care of you and your family. Always, sweet Elena."

"You love me," she said.

"Aye," he said. "I love you. I want you to be my wife."

She smiled at him and touched his face gently. "I want to be your wife."

An enormous grin crossed his face and she laughed when he said, "Aye, of course you do. Why would you not?"

He laid down beside her and rested his hand on her belly. "Do you want a boy or a girl, sweet Elena?"

"Traven, it will take a few weeks for the effects of the tea to leave my body. I am not with child yet."

"Aye, I know. But do you want a boy or a girl first?"

"A boy," she said. "A boy with green eyes, who will grow big and strong like his father. What about you?"

"It does not matter to me," he said before kissing her again. "I am happy for either. I love you, Elena."

"I love you, Traven."

CHAPTER 15

"Bonnie?"

"Get away from me, lord Graham." Bonnie stalked down the hallway toward her room.

He followed her and shoved his way into her room when she tried to slam the door in his face.

"I said leave! I no longer wish to sleep with you," Bonnie said furiously.

"Bonnie, I am sorry." He pulled her struggling body into his arms, wrapping his arms around her and holding her tight. He pressed kisses across her throat. "I am so sorry, little Bonnie. But I had no choice. If I had pleaded for mercy for you, Traven would have been immediately suspicious of my actions. I am not, by nature, a merciful man."

"No, you are not," she spat at him.

He sighed and rested his forehead against hers. "I am truly sorry, my Bonnie. Truly. But I will admit that there was a large part of me that wondered why you were still stealing. We had an agreement, you and I, did we not? You no longer need to practice acts of thievery, I will always take care of you."

"Like you did earlier when I almost lost my hand? If it were not for Elena, I would have a stump for a right hand and be out on the street by now."

"I am sorry," he repeated. His voice was low and the genuine remorse in it made her pause and study his face.

"I swore to you I would look after you and I failed you," he admitted. "But you have not answered me as to why you kept stealing."

She sighed. "I-I was not certain you would keep your word to me, lord Graham."

"I understand," he pressed a kiss against her mouth, "but I will always take care of you."

"You did not earlier," she said. "I do not think I can help you with your plan, my lord. It does not seem right after lord Traven showed me mercy."

A brief flicker of anger flared in his eyes before he gave her a somber smile. "Aye, I understand."

He kissed her before releasing her and walking toward the door. He paused and turned to face her. "Bonnie, you realize that Elena was only using you, do you not?"

"What do you mean?" She asked.

He sighed wearily and trudged back to her. "Little Bonnie, you are so naïve, sometimes. If Elena carries Traven's child, he will marry her. He bends to her will now, which means she will be in charge. Do you honestly think she will keep you in their home?"

"She helped me," Bonnie whispered.

"Aye, she did," Graham replied. "She helped you only in a bid to bargain her way back into Traven's bed. And it worked, did it not?"

"Aye," Bonnie whispered again.

Graham stroked her cheek with his thumb. "Once she is

Traven's wife, she will kick us and anyone else who dares to defy her out of Traven's home."

"She would not do that. Elena is kind and -"

Graham gave her a little shake. "Use your head, Bonnie. You are a kind girl. If it was you who bore Traven's ring and his collar, would you allow a servant who had pleasured him to remain in the home?"

"No," Bonnie said in a low voice.

"Exactly." Graham held up a small glass vial, the blue liquid inside of it shone in the flickering candlelight. "I will not ask you to do something you do not want to do, little Bonnie. But if you are clever, you will pour this into Traven's drink tomorrow night."

He kissed her forehead. "Before there is any chance that Elena carries his child."

Bonnie stared at the vial before slowly taking it from his hand. She tucked it into her pocket and Graham smiled at her. "That is my good girl. You have made the right choice, little Bonnie."

TRAVEN RESTED HIS HAND ON ELENA'S THIGH. SHE WAS sitting beside him staring into the fire and he squeezed her knee. "Are you all right, my love?"

"Aye," she said. "I am content."

"As am I." He picked up her hand and kissed her knuckles as Duncan joined them.

He sat down in the chair on the other side of Traven. "Good evening."

"Hello, Duncan," Traven replied. "Where have you been all day? I have not seen you since Elena's family left this morning."

"In the stables, mostly," Duncan replied. "I am teaching Bryce how to fight with the sword."

"He is so young," Elena said. "Are you certain he is ready?"

"Aye," Duncan said. "Your family seemed eager to leave this morning."

"They did," Elena said with a small smile. "The news of my engagement to Traven was not well received, I am afraid."

Duncan laughed before glancing around the crowded common room. "Everyone else seems to be happy enough."

"Almost everyone," Traven replied. His gaze crossed the room to where Graham sat at the table. He was staring moodily into a glass of mead and paying no attention to the others in the room. "Graham congratulated us both, but I do not believe his heart was in it. Do you, Elena?"

She shook her head as Duncan shrugged. "It is not surprising."

"No, I suppose not," Traven said with a heavy sigh.

He looked up as Bonnie approached them. She held a tray with three glasses of mead, and she gave one to Duncan, one to Elena and the final one to him. "My lord, I bring you a drink to show you my gratitude for your mercy."

"That is kind of you, Bonnie." Traven took the glass from her as Graham appeared. "Graham, old friend, you are so somber tonight. Life is too short to be so bleak. This is a day of celebration. Will you join me for a drink?"

"Aye, Traven, I will," Graham said.

"Good." Traven held up his glass of mead as the others did the same. "To old friends and new beginnings."

He glanced at Elena who smiled at him. He grinned at her and took a long drink of the cold mead before wiping the foam from his upper lip. He turned to Graham. The man's somber look had been replaced with a large smile and he held his glass out to Traven again. "To you, Traven. May you live a long and healthy life."

"Aye, the same to you, Graham." Traven took another drink. "You suddenly seem much happier, my friend."

Graham grinned at him. "Because I see the wisdom of your words, Traven. Life is too short to keep such melancholy thoughts in my heart."

Duncan stood and, without speaking, brushed past Graham and joined David and Aldina who were standing a few feet away.

"Aye." Traven set the glass down before resting his hand on Elena's thigh. "Or perhaps your sudden change in disposition is because of the poison you believe is in my drink."

Graham's mouth dropped open and he glanced at Bonnie who was standing to his left. Her face was pale except for two red spots high on her cheeks.

"Lord Traven," Graham said. "I do not know what you speak of."

"Do you not?" Traven cocked his head at him. "So, you did not give Bonnie the poison to slip into my drink?"

"Whatever this vile, jealous little creature has said to you is a lie!" Graham snapped. "She wishes to have you for herself and will do anything to achieve her goal."

He lunged toward Bonnie, his fist raised, but stumbled to a stop when Duncan stepped between them. His sword was out, and he tapped Graham on the chest before smiling at him. "Take one more step, lord Barten, and give me a reason to use my blade."

Graham swallowed compulsively and backed up a step before staring at Traven. "My lord, I swear to you, I had nothing to do with this. I am your most loyal friend. I have done nothing but help you and -"

"Enough." Traven wanted to be angry, but instead he felt only a bitter weariness. "I know the truth, Graham. For once in your life, be a man and admit what you have done."

Graham's nostrils flared. "You are weak, Traven. Weak and useless. This was an act of mercy on my part. You are no longer the man you were. You are failing your people and you do not even care. I kept your lands from being pillaged and taken while you fought a war that meant nothing. Your people are safe and alive today because of me. I am the one who should be leading them."

"So, you turned to murder? We have been friends since we were children, Graham. I trusted you and you have betrayed that trust." Traven took a deep breath and gave Graham a look of sorrow. "You leave me no choice, old friend. Your punishment is death."

Graham stumbled back, his gaze flickering from Traven to Elena. "Lord Traven, we – you said it yourself, we have known each other for many years. Will you now show your oldest friend mercy for a mistake he has made?"

"A mistake," Traven said. "You call trying to murder me a mistake?"

Graham's face paled and he fell on his knees in front of Elena. "My lady, please. You are a kind woman. If you ask him, he will grant me mercy. I know it."

Elena placed her hand on Traven's where it still rested on her thigh. "Lord Barten, you ask me for mercy?"

"Aye, I do, Elena. Remember, I was the one who hired you and your William to work here. I allowed you to escape from your wretched family and start fresh with your husband."

"Aye, you did," Elena said. "Until you killed my William."

Traven watched as the colour drained from Graham's

face. Graham glanced at Bonnie who gave him a solemn look. "Aye, I told her everything."

Graham's throat worked compulsively before he croaked out. "The girl lies. I did not poison your husband, my lady."

"You did," Elena said softly. "You murdered my husband and tonight, you tried to murder Traven, the man I love more than anything else in this world."

She leaned forward and studied Graham. "I will show you no mercy."

ELENA PICKED HER WAY ACROSS THE MUDDY GROUND. THE weather had warmed in the last few days and the mud was thick and dark. She hadn't even needed her cloak, although from the way Traven was staring at her, she was certain she was about to receive a lecture.

"Elena," he said when she joined him and Duncan. "It may be spring, but it is still cool. Where is your cloak? In your condition, it would not be wise for you to catch a chill."

She grinned up at him. "I am fine, my lord. You worry too much."

She glanced at the wall that surrounded the estate, studying Graham's decaying head that was impaled on one of the spikes, and poked Traven in the side. "My lord, perhaps it is time to take that down. It has been there all winter."

Traven grinned at her. "It is a good reminder to others of what will happen to those who betray me."

"Aye, but perhaps you could take it down before our child is born."

Traven rubbed her belly, his smile growing large. "Aye, I could do that. I will ask Jameson to take it down this afternoon."

"Thank you, my lord." She turned to Duncan, the smile sliding from her face as she studied the pack on his back. "Duncan, are you certain this is what you want to do?"

"Aye, Elena, I am," Duncan replied.

She sighed and hugged him tightly. "I am going to miss you."

"I will miss you too," he said.

"Are you sure you will not take a horse?" She asked.

He shook his head. "No, I need to walk."

She frowned at him. "You should take a horse."

"If I get tired of walking, I will buy one," he said.

She laughed and gave his hand a quick squeeze. "Will you write?"

"I will try."

"That means no," Traven said. "After today, we will never see or hear from you again."

Elena watched the myriad of emotions cross Traven's face. Sorrow, anxiety and anger were most prominent.

"Duncan," Traven said urgently, "you should think longer on your decision."

"I have thought long enough, my friend," Duncan said. "This is what I need to do."

Traven sighed, his shoulders slumping. "Aye, I know. I hope you find what you are looking for, old friend."

"I will," Duncan said.

The two men hugged for a long moment before breaking apart. Duncan cleared his throat roughly and smiled at them. "I am more happy than I can say for the both of you. Take care of each other, all right?"

"Aye, we will, Duncan. Be careful," Elena said.

"I will." Duncan took a deep breath before smiling at Traven. "Good bye, Traven."

"Good bye, Duncan."

Elena took Traven's hand as Duncan turned and walked toward the gate. Jameson opened it and Duncan turned and waved at them. They waved back and he smiled before adjusting his pack and walking through the open gate.

As the gate closed slowly behind him, Elena stared up at Traven. "I am sorry, my love. I know how much you will miss him."

She reached up and wiped the moisture from his cheeks as he stared down at her. "He must find his own path and as much as I want him to stay, I cannot force him to remain here."

"No, you cannot," she said.

He sighed and she wrapped her arms around his waist before kissing his chest. "Come, my lord, your breakfast awaits and – oh!"

Traven grinned and rested his big hand on her belly. "I felt that one."

She laughed and rubbed her belly. "I am not surprised. Your child has grown quite adept at kicking me."

He leaned down and kissed her swollen belly. "He is his father's son."

"Or daughter," she said.

"Or daughter," he agreed before pressing a kiss against her mouth. "I love you, sweet Elena."

"I love you too, Traven."

"DUNCAN, YOU FOOL," HE MUTTERED TO HIMSELF. "YOU should have stayed another night at the inn."

He should have. Even this morning, the dark clouds had begun to roll across the sky and the old man who ran the inn had warned him that a storm was coming.

Anxious to be on his way, Duncan had ignored his urging to stay another night and continued on his journey. A decision he was regretting now.

He squinted in the rain as the wind whipped his cloak around his body like a wet blanket. The water was seeping into his pack and every part of him was wet and cold and miserable. He kept his hand on the handle of his sword that hung around his waist.

He doubted very much that any one else, human or animal, would be out in this storm, but he was taking no chances. This part of the country was known for its thieves and murderers and he had no wish to die just because he was distracted by a little rain.

A little rain? This is more than a little rain, Duncan. Something is not right about this storm, you can feel it.

He could feel it. An electricity in the air that made the hair on the back of his neck stand up and little alarm bells go off inside his body. He squinted again into the darkness. He could barely see the road that wound through the forest.

A sudden gust of wind staggered him on his feet. If the wind grew any stronger, he would have to lash himself to a tree just to keep from blowing away. Thunder boomed over-head and lightning flashed across the sky, lighting up the forest around him.

He winced and bent his head against the wind. He needed to find shelter fast before…

He stared in surprise at his hand. He could see the rain splashing against it, even see the small cut on his palm. The lightning was gone, so why was the darkness disappearing?

He glanced up, his mouth dropping open at the sight of the small glowing orb directly in front of him. It pulsed with light and it grew larger by the second. The wind was howling now, nearly pushing him toward the light and he staggered back a few steps.

Something was wrong with that light. Something terribly wrong and he needed to get away from it.

He turned and ran, but the wind was a howling, menacing force that refused to let him flee. He dug his feet in, his eyes widening in surprise when they slid backward across the mud-covered road. He took a quick glance behind him, the shout of alarm dying on his lips. The orb was huge now, taller than him and as wide as the road. The light pulsated and throbbed, a humming sound made his ears pop painfully and he made no sound at all when the light wrapped around him with a blinding, pulsing wave of energy and he was sucked into the orb.

There was darkness and for a moment he wondered if he was blind and deaf or... dead. A wave of dizziness rushed over him, his body felt like it was on the verge of tearing apart and he screamed silently into the black void as blinding pain filled every molecule.

He landed hard on the spongy ground, his shoulder and hip taking the brunt of his landing. He kept his eyes closed, his breathing harsh in his ears, his entire body trembling. After a few minutes, he sat up and opened his eyes.

"What..." he whispered, staring in shock at his surroundings.

The air was moist and humid, he could hear the strange cries of birds above his head, and lush vegetation surrounded him. He reached out and touched the broad green leaf of a plant closest to him as a bug, it was the size of his hand and bright green in colour, lumbered up the trunk of the tree behind the plant.

He had never seen a creature like it before and the alarm bells were back, racing up and down his spine, sending a rush of adrenaline to his bruised body. He stood, his knees buckled, and he caught himself on the trunk of the tree before straightening. He touched the comforting weight of the sword around his waist as the rain, now just a drizzle, stopped completely. He glanced behind him, his eyes widening again. He staggered forward to the edge of the cliff and his jaw dropped.

"What is this place?" He whispered as he stared at the vast expanse of water that went as far as his eye could see. Huge waves crashed into the rocks that jutted out below him and he watched in fascination.

The sound of a branch breaking behind him broke the spell of the water and he whirled around, yanking his sword from its sheath around his waist. He stared silently at the two men standing behind him. Both were large and muscular, and they wore the strangest clothing he had ever seen. Their shirts were dark green, and their pants had an odd combination of green and brown splotches all over them.

They both held small metal objects in their hands that they kept pointed at his chest. The bigger one, his arms were covered in strange markings, looked him up and down. "What's your name?"

Duncan didn't reply and the second one said, "Teagan, he has a goddamn sword. Do you see that thing?"

"I see it," Teagan replied. "What's your name? Answer me or I'll shoot you in the fucking head."

"Dude, chill out," the second man said. "Garrett sent us on a find and retrieve mission, not a murder spree." He glanced behind him. "Maybe the guy doesn't speak English."

He turned back to Duncan. "Hey… hablas Espanol?"

The other man rolled his eyes. "Even if he did speak Spanish, that's the only fucking phrase you know, Wallace."

"What is this place?" Duncan said.

"He speaks English!" Wallace held out his fist to Teagan. "Fuckin' A, right?"

Teagan ignored him and stared at Duncan. "Put down that sword and come with us."

"I think not," Duncan said. "You have no sword and I am," he paused, "quite adept at the blade."

"Jesus, he doesn't know what a fucking gun is," Wallace said. "Teag, he's from the middle ages, he's gotta be, right? Look at the way he's dressed and he's carrying a fucking sword."

"Yeah," Teagan said. He glanced behind him before touching the wreath of yellow flowers that hung around his neck. "We need to get moving before the pinkies show up."

"Yeah, you're telling me." The one named Wallace lowered the strange metal object in his hand and stuck out his other hand. "I'm Wallace and this is Teagan. What's your name?"

"Duncan." He studied the man's outstretched hand.

Wallace elbowed Teagan. "Lower your gun, man."

Teagan lowered his hand and Duncan lowered his sword and took a few steps forward. He shook Wallace's hand before glancing around. "What is this place?"

Wallace grinned at him. "Welcome to hell, brother."

A Note for my Amazing Readers.

Hello!

. . .

IF YOU'VE BEEN READING THE OTHER WORLD SERIES FROM the beginning, then no doubt you have realized who Duncan is and that you first met him in Book Six "Choosing Rose". As I was writing "Choosing Rose", I had no intention of writing an origin story for Duncan, but halfway through it, I realized that Duncan (more so his best friend Traven) were shouting quite vehemently that they needed their own book.

I ignored them for a few weeks, pointing out to them repeatedly that writing an origin story did not fit into the narrative or direction of the series. They were insistent though, and one night, long after my husband had gone to bed and Dexter the mutant chihuahua was asleep in his bed at my feet, I could no longer ignore their calls for attention. I began writing the story and never looked back.

So, where does this leave us? For those of you who have read every book in the series, you're luckily in a position where you won't be confused with how the next book after Elena Unbound starts.

But for those of you who have read only this book, it could be quite confusing. If you loved Duncan and want to read more about him, then I would suggest reading Book Six in the series, entitled "Choosing Rose". Duncan is only a secondary character in the book (and it takes a bit for him to show up), but it explains what happens to him after he was sucked into the orb and meets Teagan and Wallace in the jungle, and will give you a better understanding of the next book in the series that follows Elena Unbound.

THANK YOU FOR READING ELENA UNBOUND. PLEASE READ ON for an excerpt of the next book in the series!

BOOK EIGHT EXCERPT

(OTHER WORLD SERIES BOOK EIGHT)

The cold was all around him, surrounding him in a thick, heavy blanket that stole his breath and numbed his extremities. Hard pellets of snow struck his skin, leaving miniscule red dots that burned. Wallace staggered to his feet, his stomach still churning from the journey through the orb, and he stared in solemn surprise at the new world.

"Holy motherfucking shit cakes. We're on the goddamn planet of Hoth. Teag, are you seeing this shit? Are you feeling this shit? How long has it been since you felt fucking cold? Because I gotta tell you…"

He turned, tension radiating through his chest when he realized he was alone. The blizzard of snow and ice hadn't abated with the disappearance of the orb and he took a few steps forward. Maybe Teagan and Duncan were only a few feet away and he just couldn't see them thanks to the fucking blizzard.

"Teagan? Teag, man, don't fuck around!" He could hear the panic in his voice. "Where are you guys?"

There was nothing but the howling of the wind and he cupped his hands around his mouth and shouted, "Teagan! Duncan! Answer me, goddammit!"

Still nothing and the panic turned to fear. He ran forward blindly, shouting both Teagan and Duncan's name, the wind still howling and the snow pelting his skin.

He stumbled to a stop and stared up at the sky before screaming his rage. "Are you fucking kidding me?"

He screamed repeatedly before sinking to his knees in the shin deep snow. He was shivering and shaking with cold and already his hands were so numb he couldn't feel them. He stuck them into his armpits as he squinted into the blizzard.

"Gotta find shelter," he mumbled. "I can't believe I'm gonna fucking freeze to death after spending five fucking years sweating my nutsack off on a goddamn island. That's some fucking funny joke."

Wallace, move! You have to keep moving before you freeze to death.

His inner voice was right, but he had a feeling he was already about ten minutes away from dying. He'd grown up on a farm in South Dakota and thought he'd known what cold was.

"Wrong again, asshole," he muttered before staggering to his feet. "This isn't just cold, this is…"

Death?

"Probably," he groaned before forcing himself to stagger forward. His t-shirt and pants did nothing to cut the cold wind and within minutes a thin layer of ice had formed below his nose and along his eyelashes.

Another five minutes and his numb body could walk no further. He fell to his knees again, his pack heavy with snow and ice, and bowed his head.

He was starting to feel warmer and his body was no

longer shivering. He frowned a little. Fuck, hypothermia was setting in already.

"Wallace! Wallace, the cows are out again!"

He peered into the snow at the shadowy figure who was walking toward him. "Mama? What are you doing on Hoth? You hate Star Wars."

"Get up, Wallace. The cows are out, and your father needs your help."

"Can't," he whispered. "I'm too cold, Mama."

He fell face forward into the snow, groaning when he was turned onto his back. He peered up at the woman bending over him. Her skin was smooth and pale, and he could see tendrils of blonde hair peeking out from the hood of her fur-lined coat. Bright blue eyes, the colour of the sky at home, stared solemnly at him and she had the cutest row of freckles across the bridge of her nose. She was, he decided, the most beautiful woman he'd ever seen in his life.

As darkness edged across his vision, he croaked, "Are you an angel?"

She leaned even closer and inhaled deeply before a smile broke across her face. She had even white teeth and he studied her eyeteeth. They were slightly longer and... were those fangs?

"You are... human," she said as her fangs lengthened.

Wallace groaned. "Oh, fuck me side..."

The darkness descended fully.

Please keep reading for an excerpt from the first book in Ramona Gray's romantic suspense shifter series, Shadow Security Series

DEAD OF NIGHT EXCERPT

(BOOK ONE, SHADOW SECURITY)

———

Ryleigh leaned back in her chair, studying the crowd of people milling about the café. She stroked absently at the dark wig she was wearing. "How good do you think these guys are at their job?"

"What do you mean?" Ryan asked.

Ryleigh shrugged. "Just wondering if they're worth the money that Grandmother is shelling out."

"Whatever you're thinking, stop," Ryan said as fresh alarm bells went off in her head.

An impish grin crossed Ryleigh's face. "There's no harm in finding out if they're worth the cost, Ry-Ry."

"Ryleigh, don't -"

Ryleigh pulled off the dark wig she was wearing with a flourish and sat it on the table. Her long blonde hair was in a low bun and she pulled out the elastic, smoothing her hair before taking off her glasses and setting them next to the wig.

Her smile widened as she waved at the woman who had slowed to a stop next to their table. "Oh my God, are you... are you Ryleigh Shepherd?"

"I sure am," Ryleigh said.

"Oh my God, I love you!" The woman squealed like a rusty hinge, the sound drilling into Ryan's skull.

"Aren't you sweet," Ryleigh cocked her head at her. "Would you like an autograph?"

"Yes! Oh my God, yes! Oh shit, I need paper. I need some paper! Who has paper?" The woman's voice was shrill and eager, and Ryan muttered a curse when everyone in the coffee shop looked their way.

There was a collective gasp, a murmur of excitement went through the crowd, and Ryleigh's grin grew.

"Here we go," she said to Ryan.

"Oh fuck," Ryan said as the people surged toward them.

She stood up as Ryleigh did, trying to reach for her sister's hand, but there was already a herd of tourists surrounding her.

Frantic shouts filled the shop as more and more people crowded closer. Cameras were behind held up in the air as people tried to get a picture of Ryleigh.

A woman, her face bright red, grabbed a handful of Ryleigh's hair and yanked on it. Ryleigh cried out in pain as the woman squealed to another woman behind her, "Holy shit, it's real! I thought it was a wig, swear to God, Jennifer! It ain't a wig!"

"Ryan!" The fear in Ryleigh's voice cut through the growing panic in Ryan's chest. She fought to get to her sister, but the flood of people was crushing her. She was trapped between a sweaty, foul-smelling man wearing a trucker hat and a woman in a flowered dress wearing so much perfume it practically dripped from her pores.

She cried out when the woman, her hands jerking wildly in excitement, scratched her across the cheek. There was stinging pain and liquid dripped down her cheek. The man in the trucker hat raised his arms and bellowed Ryleigh's name as he surged forward. The man in front of him turned and shoved him back. Sweaty man stumbled, his elbow slamming into the side of Ryan's face.

Little flashes of light swarmed across her vision and she was immediately lightheaded. Her cheek throbbed in agony and she swallowed down bile as she shook her head. More pain flooded through her.

She was going to die in a goddamn coffee shop. Squashed to death between a woman who'd bathed in Obsession by Calvin Klein and a man who hadn't bathed since God was a baby.

"Move!"

The loud and angry growl was a soothing balm to her ears. The perfume-laden woman was jostled aside, and Ryan flailed for Grayson's wide shoulders like a woman drowning. He slipped an arm around her waist and pulled her up against him, his big body protecting her from the riot of tourists.

"Ryleigh!" Ryan gasped out when Grayson lifted her into his arms. "Help Ryleigh first!"

Grayson ignored her, turning and pushing his way through the crowd of people. She tried to get free, wiggling and squirming in his arms.

He squeezed her tight and growled, "Stay still."

"Ryleigh! You need to help Ryleigh!"

"Chase and Wes will help her."

"No!" She stared at him in panic as he kicked open the door to the coffee shop and carried her out into the bright sunlight. "Grayson, go back!"

Still ignoring her, he carried her to the SUV. He set her on her feet, clamping one arm around her waist when she tried to run back toward the café, and opened the back-passenger door before lifting her and tossing her inside. He climbed in beside her and slid across the seat when she immediately scrambled to open the opposite door. He grabbed her wrist.

"Ryan, enough!"

"Ryleigh needs help! Let go of me."

"Enough!" His angry growl made her freeze in place. He cupped the back of her neck again and slid closer until her back was pressed against the door and their faces were only inches apart.

"Please help her," she whispered.

"My job is to protect you." His voice was raspy, and his eyes had turned a bright jade, their pupils narrow slits as he stared directly at her.

There was the loud roar of an angry cat, and Ryan winced as Grayson looked out the windshield. "Stay here."

He opened the back door and jumped out. Ryan cried out with relief when she saw Chase with Ryleigh in his arms, running across the parking lot toward them. He dumped her on the seat next to Ryan and climbed in after her. Grayson ripped open the driver's side door and slid behind the wheel.

"Where's Wes?" He started the vehicle as Chase slammed the back door shut.

"Holding back the crowd," Chase said. He was panting and his dark eyes had turned bright yellow. "He should be... there he is!"

Ryan watched with wide-eyed panic as Wes came busting out of the front door of the coffee shop. He ran across the lot as Grayson leaned over and opened the door. He threw the SUV into reverse and stepped on the gas as Wes shot into the car like a bullet. He slammed the door shut and Grayson put the car into drive as the horde of tourists ran across the parking lot, screaming Ryleigh's name.

"Go, Grayson, go!" Chase shouted.

Grayson tore out of the parking lot and onto the street, barely missing a blue Camaro. The Camaro's driver honked his horn and stuck his hand out the sunroof, his middle finger jabbing into the air, the gigantic fuck you a testament to Grayson's wild driving. Ignoring him, Grayson stepped on the gas, leaving the café and the crowd of tourists behind them.

"Ryleigh, sweetie, are you okay?" Ryan scanned Ryleigh's face and body, adrenaline making her voice too loud and too high.

"Yeah, I'm okay. I'm fine," Ryleigh whispered and then burst into tears.

Ryan pulled her into her arms, hugging her hard and kissing the top of her head. "You're all right, sweetie."

She rocked Ryleigh back and forth as Chase leaned against the back of the seat. His shirt was ripped, and he rubbed at the top of his skull. "Fuck, some woman ripped out a chunk of my hair when I was picking up Ryleigh. Thank fucking Christ we brought Wes with us. We wouldn't have gotten out of there alive. What the fuck is wrong with people?"

He took a deep breath before reaching out and squeezing Wes's shoulder. "You okay, man?"

Ryan studied the older man as Ryleigh sobbed quietly into her shoulder. His shirt was hanging in tatters around his body and she could see red scratches across his arms.

"I'm good," he said.

"You sure?" Grayson gave his destroyed shirt a quick glance.

"Yeah, there were two women at the front of the mob who

scratched my arms up some, but they didn't do this to my shirt. I almost had to shift to keep them back once we got Ryleigh out of the cafe."

"Fuck," Chase said. "Did you see that cougar shifter completely lose it? She shifted and tore some guy's leg open trying to jump over him to get to Ryleigh."

"Yeah, I saw it," Wes said.

Sirens wailed in the distance. Grayson stared at Ryan and Ryleigh in the rear-view mirror. Her sister's quiet sobs had slowed to the occasional sniffle. "What the fuck were you thinking taking off your disguise?"

"I'm sorry," Ryleigh whispered. "I wasn't – I mean, I didn't think…"

"No, you didn't think," Grayson snapped. "You acted impulsively, and you almost got your sister crushed to death by a mob of people."

"Stop it, Grayson," Ryan said.

"Do you have any idea how close you just came to seriously injuring or killing your sister?" Grayson carried on relentlessly.

"They were hurting me too," Ryleigh whispered.

Grayson snarled at her, his eyes flashing bright jade. "And whose fault is that?"

"Gray," Wes said quietly.

"She needs to understand that there are consequences to her actions," Grayson growled.

"I didn't mean to do it, okay?" Ryleigh started to cry again, throwing herself into Ryan's arms. "Ry-Ry, it was an accident."

"I know," Ryan said, "I know it was, sweetie. It's -"

"Don't you dare tell her it's all right," Grayson said. His hands gripped the steering wheel until it creaked. "She could have gotten you killed, Ryan."

"It was an accident." Ryan glared at him as Ryleigh sobbed harder. "Let it go, Grayson."

"Let it go? Ryan, you -"

"Enough, Gray." Wes's hand landed on his shoulder hard enough to make Grayson wince. "We can talk about this later when everyone's calmed down."

Grayson stared grimly at Ryan in the rear-view mirror. She returned his look for a few seconds before turning and staring out the window as Ryleigh continued to sob in her arms.

ABOUT THE AUTHOR

Ramona Gray is a Canadian romance author. She currently lives in Alberta with her awesome husband and her super cute dog. She's addicted to home improvement shows, good coffee, and reading and writing about the steamier moments in life.

For more information about Ramona, check out her website at

www.ramonagray.ca

ALSO BY RAMONA GRAY

Individual Books

The Escort

Saving Jax

The Assistant

One Night

Sharing Del

Filthy Appeal

Forbidden Bliss

Shadow Security Series

Dead of Night

Edge of Night

Dark of Night

Undeniable Series

Undeniably His

Undeniably Hers

Undeniably Theirs

Undeniable Series Boxset

Working Men Series

The Mechanic

The Carpenter

The Bartender

The Welder

The Electrician

The Landscaper

The Firefighter

The Cop

The Paramedic

Working Men Series Bundles

Working Men Series Books One to Three

Working Men Series Books Four to Six

Working Men Series Books Seven to Nine

Other World Series

The Vampire's Kiss (Book One)

The Vampire's Love (Book Two)

The Shifter's Mate (Book Three)

Rescued By The Wolf (Book Four)

Claiming Quinn (Book Five)

Choosing Rose (Book Six)

Elena Unbound (Book Seven)

Other World Series Box Sets

Other World Series Books One to Three

Other World Series Books Four to Six

www.ingramcontent.com/pod-product-compliance
Lightning Source LLC
Chambersburg PA
CBHW071255250626
47159CB00004B/1195